The Brides of Solomon

and Other Stories

The Brides of Solomon
and Other Stories

Geoffrey Household

An Atlantic Monthly Press Book

Little, Brown and Company · Boston · Toronto

ATLANTIC—LITTLE, BROWN BOOKS
ARE PUBLISHED BY
LITTLE, BROWN AND COMPANY
IN ASSOCIATION WITH
THE ATLANTIC MONTHLY PRESS

*Published simultaneously in Canada
by Little, Brown & Company (Canada) Limited*

PRINTED IN THE UNITED STATES OF AMERICA

For Nyusi and Nicky

Contents

The Brides of Solomon

and Other Stories

The Case of Valentin Lecormier

M. LE CONSUL:

I ask you to excuse the paper upon which this is written. Where I am, the necessities of civilization do not exist. Even the poor devils of police who patrol the frontier do not normally carry paper. In order to write to you I had to capture an assistant inspector of customs, and relieve him of his spare account books.

This is not a begging letter. You cannot help me. Whether I live or die depends entirely on myself, and I do not know which I deserve. In any case one rarely receives what one merits. No, M. le Consul, I write to you only to establish the nationality of my wife and children.

We were married by the priest of Ferjeyn on April 15, 1944. The marriage is recorded in the church register, and also the births of my three sons. They are French and, though so young, they know it. In twelve years they will be ready and willing for their military service. I shall be grateful to you if you will enter their names upon the register of French citizens. As for my wife, she is a simple Christian Arab. Syria is her country, and without me she would be lost in France.

M. le Consul, my name is Valentin Lecormier, formerly sergeant-major of cavalry. I am a deserter. It is very rare for a warrant officer of the regular army to desert, but I will explain it as best I can. There may be some record of me in your office files, but it is probably considered that I am dead.

I joined the Army in 1932. For me it was a profession as congenial as any other, and, to tell you the truth, what most attracted me was the pleasant life of our little garrison towns. I was not such a fool, of course, as to suppose that I should spend all my years of service under the trees of the main square; but we export our civilization with our soldiers, and I knew that I should seldom be far from a shaded pavement upon which to spend my hours of leisure.

When that damned Hitler unleashed his war, I had already passed four years in Beirut as a corporal-instructor training Arab levies. I assure you I had no ambition. I merely applied for every post which suited my taste for small towns, and pretended to have the requisite qualifications. I persuaded my superiors that I spoke Arabic. And if you are young and make a show of an accomplishment which you wish you had, it will not be long before in fact you have it. That's life.

After the fall of France, when our army and government in Syria declared for Vichy, I rode over into Palestine with my troop to join the Fighting French. It was not a question of choice. I have never made a choice for myself more than any other man. Choice? There is no such thing. One follows events, and gets out of the mess as best one can. That is, I believe, what they now call existentialism. A long word for the practical philosophy of every soldier.

No, I did not trouble my head with de Gaulle or Pétain, or

faith in France or the lack of it. I considered only my affection for Colonel Collet. A mountebank. One admitted it. Still, a soldier must feel love like the rest of us, and he cannot be held responsible for where he places it.

After that there was no time for decisions. The campaign against our own countrymen in Syria. A harsh interval while we exchanged our horses for armored cars. The Western Desert. Bir Hachim. And believe me, M. le Consul, the world was wrong to make such a fuss of that battle. I was there, and I tell you we could not run away because the Boches were all round us. And then it was hardly decent to surrender when there had been so much surrendering in France.

And so, better men being dead, I was hoisted up to squadron sergeant-major, and on we went to Tripoli (where one saw a town and a square and a civilized café again) and into Italy and back to Syria for rest and reorganization.

In that narrow strip of Syria between Turkey and Iraq which is called the Duck's Bill from its shape, there was some fear of a rising of Moslem fanatics. So they sent me out in charge of a detachment. A captain was in command, of course, but an old soldier was needed to see that he came to no harm. Since I now spoke fluent Arabic, it was an excuse to present myself with a deal of liberty. I used to pass my days at Ferjeyn, which, being an island of Christians set upon a mountain in the middle of two hundred thousand Moslems, was the right post for a man of tact.

At Ferjeyn, M. le Consul, I fell in love. She was the daughter of the headman, John Douaihy. What else could you expect, given eight years of foreign service and no hope of

France? Our regiment had not been picked for the invasion — for there were not enough of us left to be any use to a higher formation — and so we comforted ourselves with the thought that it could not possibly succeed. I repeat, we had no hope of France.

I should not like you to think that my love for Helena Douaihy was that of a soldier who marries, in a moment of supreme boredom with interminable male society, the first decent girl he has seduced. No, as a responsible warrant officer, I used to warn my lads against such unsuitable attachments.

I did not seduce her. I have nothing of which to accuse myself but the strange and bitter chivalry of the French. Since it has persisted in our nation through five centuries of common sense, it is not surprising that in a poor devil like myself it should outlive those many years when my only choice was between celibacy and army prostitutes.

It was her rags, I believe, that aroused in me an overwhelming desire to cherish her. Her father was by no means badly off. But you know the Arab. He does not waste money on daughters, unless they must be currycombed and clipped for church or a party. Yes, it was her rags. When Helena was working in the fields or drawing water, she seemed to me like a fifteen-year-old princess of the romances, dressed in the clouts of the kitchen maid. She had worn her one frock so long that the stuff had become threadbare over her breasts, worn away by the continual sharp pressure from within. Well, that is not a phenomenon which repeats itself in later years; but her face has kept its delicacy. I assure you that one would turn round and stare after her even in the streets of Paris. And she has been a wife without reproach. That is what I wish to impress on you. In her way she is a true bourgeoise, and she has helped me to bring up our sons so that France can be proud of them.

It was not then — on detachment in the Duck's Bill — that fate made of me a deserter. In the spring of 1944 we were ordered, for God knows what reason, to Cyprus, where we found ourselves among a lot of damned Englishmen and Greeks. Of the two I preferred the Greeks. They have inherited the culture of the Roman Empire, whereas the English have no idea of what a town should be.

There we were. More training. Forever training. It seemed to us that we were destined to nothing but camps, year after year of camps, till we were old and gray.

It happened, M. le Consul, that the major wished to buy some wine for the officers' mess, and I for the sergeants. The wines of Cyprus are fairly drinkable, but merchants are inclined to sell any filth in their cellars to soldiers, since the English, whose palates are rotted by beer and whisky, do not know good from bad. So we decided to go out in civilian clothes. The major pretended to be a French diplomat on leave who had rented a villa in the hills, and I — I dressed myself as any poor and decent Syrian who might be his cook or butler.

We settled down in a cellar by the quay to taste what was offered. The wines were good and, to tell you the truth, we forgot all differences of rank. The *patron* did not bother us. He slept behind his counter, and only woke up when we called for another bottle. The major was not a bad little chap, but of the right wing of the de Gaullists. He was a royalist and thought of nothing but some damned Henry V who was to come to the throne of France. As for me, I am a republican. True, the Third Republic made me vomit. But being what we are, it is the best we could do.

Well, at three in the morning we began an argument. It was foolish. A sergeant-major should not talk politics, and least of all with an officer. But he was as bored as I. We were two Frenchmen, isolated among Englishmen and Greeks, with no hope of home. I cannot remember at this distance what was said. No doubt there were faults on both sides. Our nerves were exasperated. And so I found that I had hit my commanding officer over the head with a bottle.

I examined him. I had enough experience of wounds. I said to myself that he would not die, but that he would need a comfortable week in hospital. The *patron* had not waked up. In his trade, if one is to get any sleep at all, one must not pay attention to a little noise. I bandaged my major and wrapped him in blankets, and walked out onto the quay.

M. le Consul, I had made no plan whatever. Choice, as at every turning in a man's life, was forced on me. It was that hour, with dark turning to gray, when no one takes a decision, least of all a soldier. He stands to, and obeys. As for the general who issued the orders the night before, he is fast asleep.

I walked on the deserted quay, regretting that I should never see my Helena again, for she would have married some village notable long before I came out of jail. True, they might treat me more leniently. We old soldiers of the Fighting French were charitable to one another. But the best I could hope for was the mental hospital. And indeed I had well deserved that I, a sergeant-major, should spend five years sewing rabbits upon babies' nappies under the eye of the occupational therapist.

The black mass of Lebanon showed up against the red of dawn. It was not a cloud. It stood upon eighty miles of steel sea and striped haze, and so solid it was that I prostrated myself upon the quay like a Moslem praying, and bowed my farewell to Helena and to Ferjeyn and to Asia. I must admit that I was very drunk.

Then a voice hailed me from the dock:

"Brother, that is not the direction of Mecca!"

I looked up. A caïque was drifting out on the dawn wind, her captain at the great tiller. Her sail was half hoisted, and she was painted blue and yellow. I asked the captain where he was bound.

"To Beirut," he said, "if it pleases God. Come with me, brother, and learn the difference between east and south!"

He took me for a fellow Moslem, you see. And they do not care about passports and police controls, those chaps in the caïques.

All the same, he intended a mere sailor's jest, I suppose, rather than a serious invitation. But I did not wait for him to change his mind. I would have obeyed any sensible suggestion from any quarter. I dived in, and he luffed and picked me up. I told him with much detail that I was a Turk who had escaped from an English prison. That amused him so richly that he did not ask too many questions.

And there I was condemned by a single impulsive act to the life of a deserter, and presented at the same time —

for luck cuts both ways — with a chance of permanent freedom, since it would be assumed for at least a week that I was still in Cyprus.

The west wind was fresh and steady, and by sunset we were close under the land. Part of our cargo, like that of any caïque in wartime, was contraband. In the night the captain rowed his crates ashore on the beach of Batroun. Half an hour later he had resumed his voyage to Beirut, and I was walking to the coast road through a darkness that smelled of the spring rains.

By bus and lorry — and detours on foot around the control posts of the military police — I reached Damascus, where I had banked for years the economies of my military pay. It was a little account which I had kept quiet. Not that it was dishonest. Far from it. Custom demanded that when an Arab trooper was posted to the squadron of his choice or recommended for promotion he should give a little present. That was something which everyone knew, but of which no one spoke. So it was only decent that I should not flaunt my bank account before the eyes of the military authorities.

I was sure that there would be no inquiry for me yet in Syria. After all it was only forty-eight hours since I had deserted. So I presented myself at the bank without fear. There was a clerk on duty who knew me, and it was not the first time he had seen me in civilian clothes.

The sum was small. It would not have bought a decent tobacco stall in France; but it was enough for a house and farm at Ferjeyn, and something over. Provided I presented myself as a prosperous man, well dressed and careless, I had no doubt that John Douaihy would give me his daughter. They are easily impressed, the Syrians. So long as nothing is stinted at the marriage, they do not much care what happens to a daughter after.

The journey along the edge of the desert to Hassetché was arduous. I had no papers — beyond a good French military map — and so it was essential to avoid all roads and public transport. Stained with dust and salt water as I was, I resembled the poorest of Arabs. I bought a camel and pretended to be taking it to market — always at the next town along my route. I have had charge of many animals in my time, but I tell you a camel is the only one it is impossible to love. One receives a more civilized response from an intelligent jeep. Sometimes I rode my camel and sometimes I led her. She was only a stage property and of little use to me. Perhaps she knew it.

At Hassetché I sold my camel and bought a fine pony and dressed myself decently. Then I rode to Ferjeyn and was received by John Douaihy with that superb hospitality which the Christian Arab reserves for the elder European brother — provided, of course, that he behaves like a brother. John knew what I wanted from him, though we did not yet mention it. There was a difficulty to be disposed of first. He expected me to tell him that I had had enough of the war.

I should explain to you that our commune, isolated for centuries among hostile Mohammedans, saw nothing at all disgraceful in being a deserter. No fighting had ever counted for them but the long bickering between Christian and Moslem, which in their soil was native as the mulberry. War between Christian nations was to them as irresponsible as the jealousy between the House of France and the House of Anjou must have seemed to a sensible Crusader. A free fighting man who withdrew himself from participation in any such lunacy was not to be blamed.

But why tell them at all? you will ask. Because I had to prevent them from chattering far and wide that there was a real Frenchman in Ferjeyn. If they understood that I had deserted and was wanted by the police, they would be as untruthful about my past as if I had been one of themselves. And it was not difficult for them to accept me. They think in terms of religion, not, as we do, in terms of nationality. I was Christian. I spoke Arabic. Therefore, if I wished to be, I was one of the commune. It is true that they were Maronites and I (according to that enthusiastic socialist, my father) was an atheist. But Ferjeyn and Helena were well worth a mass.

M. le Consul, I married Helena and I bought my few hectares of good land. My father-in-law — for, being headman, he had the right — gave me the identity card of a man of Ferjeyn who had gone to Morocco twenty years before and never returned. I am no longer Valentin Lecormier. I am Nadim Nassar. I permit myself to bore you with these details, since I hope that you will wish to check the truth of my story. My sons, though they bear the name of Nassar, are in fact three little Lecormiers, and, I repeat, they look to France and to you to claim them in due season.

You have no interest in a renegade? M. le Consul, I plead my long service, such as it was, and I would beg you to understand that there is not all the difference you would think between Ferjeyn and a mountain village of France. I was happier there than I have ever been. True, I was ravished by my little Helena, but ravishment is not necessarily content. I will try to tell you how I could be content and still remain a Frenchman.

Where there is stone for wall and paving, one is not wholly a barbarian. My house was well above the commune and three hundred meters below the top of the mountain. In a hard winter the lowest tongues of snow felt for the limit of my land and melted into the stone channels that irrigated my terraces. When the sluices were open, the water ran on an even slope, quite silent and without foam; but the rush was so fast and smooth that a leaf falling into the channel vanished to eternity as swiftly as a human life.

When you looked up from the plain of the Duck's Bill towards Ferjeyn, you saw nothing but stone, and strips of green. Terrace rose over terrace, and above each was the bare rock from which the earth had been stripped and packed into the narrow fields that girdled the mountain. But when you looked down from my house over the gray walls and flat roofs of Ferjeyn, there were only green tops, falling in steps, of orchard and vineyard and olive and wheat. I find that civilized, M. le Consul.

The life — well, it was a little primitive but not unfamiliar. We had our group of village notables, and the café where we gathered at the end of the day's work. True, when I first knew it, our café was nothing but a hole in a ruin furnished with bench and counter. So I set into the pavement three tables which I had made with my own hands, and planted a vine to give shade. There we played our games and drank our wine and *araq* — as good fathers of families, of course — and watched the life of the commune on the flagstones of the little square. There were John Douaihy and his brother Boulos, and the priest, the saddler, the grocer and myself.

The square was my delight. On the north side was an ancient tumble-down colonnade with a roof of red tiles supported by slender pillars of stone. It had been built by a Greek architect exiled from Constantinople to our remote province. In your travels for France, M. le Consul, you must often have lived in some alien and melancholy spot which, all the same, became a home for you because of an avenue of trees or the satisfying proportions of a single house or perhaps a garden. You will know then what I felt for our square. It was the link with my civilization.

I cannot say that outside the square the streets resembled those of France. To tell you the truth, they did not exist. The houses were separated by mud in winter and dust in summer. As an old sergeant-major with a taste for tidiness, I did my best for proper streets, but without success. All the same, I persuaded Ferjeyn to establish a rubbish dump and pay a collector and a cart. That was a triumph. Admittedly he was the village idiot, but he was the only garbage man within a hundred miles.

You will have gathered, M. le Consul, that my advice was respected. I gave it rarely. If there was anything I wished to change, I was well content to spend a patient year in changing it. Peace — that was all I asked. Peace for my Helena and myself.

After Syria was given her independence, the first thought of the simple Moslem peasants around us was to raid the

Christians. A sort of celebration. It was very natural. Had the Christians been in the majority, they would have endeavored to raid the Moslems. But the government, in those early days, was determined to be as efficient as the French. They strengthened the garrison at Hassetché, and they reminded the fanatics that Syria was a land of many religions, all with the same rights of citizenship. A massacre — even though a little one and carried out for pure sport — could not be permitted.

Then, as you know, the honeymoon ended and the politicians returned to the making of money. At Damascus there were revolutions. Over here, in the lost corner of the country, there was discontent. And with us when one is discontented, one distracts oneself by taking action. The gendarmerie is weak and scattered, and there is little to prevent a criminal from escaping into Turkey or Iraq. For my part I prefer Turkey.

Day and night Ferjeyn began to talk of danger. I have never understood how the Arabs can be called fatalists. In a crisis they are hysterical as women. One must admit that there was a little danger, but only of stones thrown, of rifles fired too high to do much damage, of a house burned and cattle stolen and a woman raped — an excitement of spirit which two of my old Arabic-speaking corporals could have extinguished by mere calm and authority!

We, the notables, met at night conspiratorially, behind closed shutters in my house or the house of John Douaihy or the priest's. That made a good impression on the village. But my venerable colleagues had no more sense than children. They wanted me to make a fortress of the mountain.

"Willingly," I answered. "If I have twenty men who shoot to kill, I will hold Ferjeyn from one harvest to the next."

Ah, yes, I could have them. What did I think? That they were no soldiers? Of course I could have them, and the boys and graybeards too. . . .

But they knew and I knew that this was all talk. The truth was that they dreamed of constructing an impassable Maginot Line, for they wished to hold Ferjeyn with the least possible bloodshed. And they were right. We were sixteen hundred men, women and children, surrounded by two hundred thousand Moslems. The only tactics by which I could hold Ferjeyn — cunning and ambush and ruthless slaughter — would have meant blood feuds with the Christians that might endure a hundred years.

When I had pointed out that even a Chinese wall would not stop Moslems unless we had men on top of it trained to kill, the priest begged me to go to Palestine and buy a tank. For him a tank was a piece of magic that would make Ferjeyn invincible. He might have been talking of a sort of beetle that could move itself and fight.

I soon had enough of these councils of war which were only exclamations. I refused to take command. I wasn't having any. I was content to eat and drink and till my land. That was my life.

They did their best to persuade me. The priest waggled his fingers at me as if I were a child he was about to baptize and told me to fight for my religion. I was polite, for I had to appear impressed. But I could not share his opinion that it was a service to God to murder Moslems. All my life I have been unwilling to anticipate the intentions of the high command.

Another night John Douaihy warned me that he and I might lose our property. He was at his most dignified; he spoke like a governor of the Bank of France. I shrugged my shoulders. What could we lose? We were not rich. And a crazy band of Moslems is not an army of occupation. They do enough damage to boast about, and then go home. They cannot take away the soil in wheelbarrows.

Then the women and children. I must defend them. That was the excitement of the saddler, who, in his old age, had married a wife nearly as pretty as Helena. Well, the appetites of raiders are not a matter upon which one should let imagination rest — unless one is the wife of an old man — but someone has to be sacrificed, and memory is short.

"Brothers," I would say to them, "let us endure the chastisement that God sends us in the firm faith that it will quickly pass — so long as we have bribed the civil administration, given feasts to Moslem notables and assured the interest of the gendarmes."

All that we had done. We knew how to look after ourselves. Without any government at all, Ferjeyn would have got on very well with its neighbors. No need of proof. We Christians had been on our mountain since the Arab conquest. The flagstones of our little square were Roman. That was the strength of my argument. I appealed to history.

But, alas, we had a government of politicians and they took a hand, withdrawing all troops from the district. Their intention was obvious. They meant to divert attention from their misdeeds by allowing a raid on the Christians, and then to punish those who were responsible. Thus they could imprison a number of their political opponents without having to admit the real reason.

Down on the plain the harvest was over and the peasants were idle in the heat. Any day the attack might come. It tried our nerves a bit. Helena would sometimes scream at me from the courtyard because I was calm. When a woman's pride in her husband is hurt, she wishes all the world to know it. It is not so very different in France. I remember the wife of a colonel who would rush out on the barrack square whenever he came back late from Paris and address him from a wholly unnecessary distance. As a result we had pity on him, and made him no more trouble than we could help.

You will say, M. le Consul, that I was unworthy of the hospitality I had received, and that I had become a coward. No, I have never been extravagantly afraid to die. But one wants to know for what. We of the Fighting French died because there was nothing much to live for, and it was easy to form the habit; but in peace that won't do. One's duty is to keep under cover.

And then I and mine were safe. I did not share Ferjeyn's hatred of the Moslems. All the surrounding country knew that I was born or had become a Frenchman, and that I was only a Maronite Christian by courtesy. A man such as I could be killed any time, free of charge, if he were disliked; but if he had won affection, he would be spared, raid or no raid. I was not a hereditary enemy to be treated according to the rules of the game; I could be judged on my merits. God knows I have few enough, but I have always made friends among the simple.

My only preparation was to buy myself a good rifle. For eight years I had had no need of arms, and I was convinced I should not need them now. Still, I took care to have a whole case of good ammunition. It is idiotic to find oneself short.

We knew twelve hours before the Moslems of the plain began to stir that the raid was coming. How? M. le Consul, the Syrians cannot tell you how they know anything at all. They tip out before you a vast manure heap of rumor. It is potentially fertile, but before it can be of use it must be spread so wide that no one can discover from what cartload the green shoot of truth has sprouted.

It was the native custom to spend only one happy hour among the Christians, attacking before dawn and leaving at sunrise. Those of us in the town who had strong stone houses, with the stables below and the living rooms above, barricaded ourselves in and demolished the outside staircases. Those who had houses of one story, more or less European and quite unfitted for defense, sent their women and children up to the top of the mountain.

Helena wanted to go with them. I forbade it — but not, I beg you to believe, as an Arab husband who receives obedience as of right. A woman, frightened or in tears — one ignores her or distracts her attention by caress and compliment. That was not my way. I treated my wife as an equal, but I did not forget that a happy child obeys without knowing it obeys. I infected her with my confidence. It may be that she was the only woman in Ferjeyn to sleep a little.

I was sure that the raiders would not waste time in climbing as high as my house. At three in the morning, however, as a sensible precaution, I stationed myself upon the high roof of a ruined storehouse from which I could command the path. There, under cover of the parapet, I could speak with any of my Mohammedan acquaintances who might be out for sport. In case my friendliness were not immediately understood, I had, of course, my rifle.

They do not come on silently, the Arabs. It was that which first made me feel disgust, both as a soldier and a European. Good God, if one wants to surprise and kill, one should move like a tiger — whereas these poor barbarians yapped like a pack of dancing jackals! They were drunk with their religion. I understood more clearly the nature of the raid. For them, it was a sort of revival meeting.

I have no patience with fanatics. I am far from the convinced atheist that my father wished me to be, but I must admit that unbelievers have their uses. A little mockery compels the religious to behave themselves. In France it is enough to set the tone of public opinion. The same for alcohol. What prevents us all from drinking ourselves incapable? The fear of ridicule.

But mockery is a townsman's weapon. That yelling mob of half-wit peasants called for something stronger. How many of them there were I could not tell. Over five hundred. Enough, at any rate, if one turned a Hotchkiss on them, to make the houris of paradise work overtime. Their torches showed the black masses skipping up the tracks to Ferjeyn, with the flankers leaping from terrace to terrace. They might have been a great herd of goats with the spring fever on them.

The two streets that led into the village were defended by our young men. I do not think I malign them if I say that the chief object of each was to escape with life and with a sword cut or two to show that he had fought bravely. That was what we had known all along, but it was indecent to admit it. They were overrun. Of Christians and Moslems there were five dead — persons of no importance who could be easily forgotten when the affair was patched up and speeches made and compensation paid. The leaders, as in our own wars, were well behind the front line. It is curious when you see a vagueness, a mere way of thought, translated into action. Ferjeyn did not mean to kill. Some defense was necessary, both for self-respect and to discourage raiding in future, but unforgivable losses had to be avoided.

The horde skipped and gamboled through our deserted streets, with their dirty rags floating behind them, and yelling for Christian blood just as we do, at times of crisis, for that of bankers or politicians. Here and there, in the light of the torches, I saw a face I knew. It was rather the shadow of a face, so distorted by frenzy as to be unrecognizable. They set fire to whatever would burn. That was not much, for the old houses of Ferjeyn had walls a meter thick. My poor village idiot was chased and sacrificed. And somewhere they burst into a house. I heard the cries of the women.

The light was growing. They did not attempt to climb to the higher farms; there was enough for them to do in Ferjeyn. They burst into our café and sacked it, breaking the bottles of *araq* and emptying out the wine barrels down the hill. Among them were drovers and peddlers who, when they came up to Ferjeyn on a friendly errand, would toss down a drink like anyone else and take the more pleasure since it was forbidden; but now our poor wine became a symbol of the unbeliever. So they tore down the whole shop, and set fire to counter, shelves and barrels in the square.

From my rooftop I could see all — the fire, the dead and the bodies of two women upon whom they had used their knives. That was their habit, and it was Ferjeyn's to forgive. There would be apologies and then peace for another twenty years. A Moslem raid was a risk of our life. In civilized countries there are worse risks and more of them. A woman who has been run over — she is not a pretty sight either.

Then they started on the church. I should have liked to see our priest stand in the doorway with his cross. That indeed would have been religion. And it might have worked. The Arabs are easily made ashamed by dignity. But he was up the mountain, comforting the women. Well, if it was not his business, it was certainly not mine.

They should have gone home, for there was light enough now to recognize every lunatic among them; but they were still not content. They began to knock down the stone pillars on the north side of the square, and to lever up the pavement. That, M. le Consul, was not religious mania. It was jealousy of our common heritage.

Do you know the Moslem villages in our corner of Syria? They are mud huts built upon a mound of their own filth, ten or twenty meters above the plain, which has accumulated through the ages. Well, that men who exist in those conditions should kill and burn and rape is very natural. It even astonishes me that they should lose patience only once or twice in a generation. But they cannot be permitted to outrage all the decencies.

In that moment I saw Ferjeyn as our possession, yours and mine. I will try to explain. It was a part of France or Italy or Spain. A little Christian town. It is true that the inhabitants were Arabs, and the society upon our square did not amount to much. Nevertheless, town square it was. And even in France one does not expect profundities from the comrades with whom one plays dominoes at the Café de la Gare.

M. le Consul, I repeat that no man can take a decision at dawn. He obeys orders and that is all. I made no choice. Being what I am, I was incapable of acting other than I did. I took, if you like, my orders from the stone. It was a part of Europe which was being violated, and that was not to be endured from barbarians who lived in mud, whose souls were brittle as mud.

I assure you that I remained calm. I was not affected by the women lying there or the child impaled upon a banner or my poor village idiot who was hardly distinguishable from his own garbage. But when they hurled down the slender drums of a pillar, I told myself it was time to act. It is true that I should have been more cautious for the sake of my wife and children. But, M. le Consul, what is the use of a family if you have not your little piece of civilization in which to put them?

I lay down regretfully upon the parapet. From the

square below, my rooftop was confused among others. They could not see who was shooting or from where. I do not pretend to be a crack shot, but I am an old soldier who can do damage even when he is under fire. Being forced into the role of avenging angel, and equally invisible, I could not miss.

First I picked off the poor fools who were tearing down the pillars, and then the banner bearers and then any man who appeared to be well dressed. That saved the government the trouble later. I had only just begun on my third clip when Ferjeyn emptied. The light was now growing faster than they could run. I shot them down on the road and in the gaps between the ranks of olives. I had for a little while the illusion that they were Boches; it was as if I were finishing the war from which I had retired. In any case there were resemblances. The peoples of the North and of the East — they have always been the enemies of our way of life.

On the edge of the plain, thinking they were out of range, they stopped to wave their bloody ironmongery and shout defiance. I bagged two more at twelve hundred meters. I blame myself. It was a waste of ammunition that I should have rebuked in a recruit.

When the sun rose I went down into the square of Ferjeyn, with my hot rifle under my arm. I might have been the only man alive. The fire was going out. The shelves and barrel staves had burned, but the counter of our café was only charred. It stood like a town altar to good humor. I do not say it had never been abused, but less than most other altars.

The banner bearers lay on the pavement, together with the child and the two women. There was also a fanatical sheik from the biggest village of the plain. He would cost Ferjeyn a shocking sum in blood money, that one. A single pillar was all we had lost. Two dead men lay among the fallen drums. And then there was the debris where they had jammed in the alleys trying to escape. Well, men being what they are, every square must be washed with blood in the course of its life, if it is to remain inviolate. I found a broken bottle with a cupful of *araq* at the bottom. That did me good.

And so up the hill to my house. Eyes no doubt were looking at me from behind barred shutters. But nobody called to me. Nobody ventured out. They did not know what to believe, or whether the raid was indeed over. They were good, simple souls, inclined to put faith in the supernatural whenever explanation was difficult. They had no means of knowing that the only saint concerned was my rifle.

I found Helena praying, with a child on each side of her and the eldest behind. All four were very stiff and imploring, like the figures in one of those pictures in the Louvre which are all red and blue and gold. I had allowed her to teach the boys what she wished. It was not right, perhaps; but I assured my conscience that the teachings of such a woman as Helena could do only good.

I told her the raid was finished, and that it was not likely to be repeated in our lifetime. I did not yet explain what had happened. She had to be allowed her moment of joy. Two or three such moments to give strength, and one can endure one's seventy years of kicks up the backside.

The boys, of course, demanded if I had killed lots of enemies. They were disappointed when I said I did not know. What do they have in their heads, those little people, that they should think killing is so difficult? And why do their eyes shine, when they themselves cannot eat a lamb killed for the Easter dinner if they have known it alive?

Well, I cleaned my rifle and made a good breakfast. I was thoughtful. As an old sergeant-major, I am naturally a bit of a politician and I began to see what was on the way to me. There are times, M. le Consul, when one apprehends with absolute certainty the fate that is approaching, yet one chooses to think it has no more reality than a bad dream.

All four of us went to work on my terraces. It is not a bad life, that, when the family works together without paying or receiving wages. Each one knows that the others — even the smallest — are doing their best. And at the end of the day there is the little town in which the father of a family can relax with his companions.

My harvest was not yet in, for on the mountain we were six weeks behind the plain. As I swung my scythe — I could not bring myself to use a sickle, like my neighbors — I wondered if I should ever eat the bread that Helena would make from our wheat. There is no bread in the world like our flat loaves. It even makes you forget the crusty rolls of France. But you will have eaten with the Christians high on Lebanon, M. le Consul, and you know.

Well, at eleven there was a civic procession to my land —

John and Boulos Douaihy, the grocer and the saddler (whose wife, no doubt, had now decided that she really had not missed much). I led them to the house. Helena brought us meat and wine, and retired. The Arab woman does not intrude on the society of men; she is perfectly capable of upsetting afterwards whatever they have decided.

We congratulated ourselves upon the courage with which we had so brilliantly dispersed the raid. We talked for an hour, showing nothing but fine Arabic and good will. But at last there was a shade of embarrassment. Not one of them knew for certain what had happened.

I explained, deprecatingly, that I had perhaps fired one or two shots and that, seeing it was the will of God, the bullets had not been wasted. They were so puzzled that they took me literally and asked who fired the others. No way out! I admitted that all were mine.

"But how many have you killed?" John asked.

He was so appalled that he forgot his manners. A direct question like that is not asked — unless, of course, one is encouraging a good storyteller to exaggerate his exploits.

"Perhaps a dozen. Perhaps two."

I had not counted. There were six in the square, all dead. There were eight where I had fired into the crowd (the wounded they had carried off). Then there were those in the orchards, who may have amounted to two dead and four able to crawl away. And, by the way they fell, I might count two as a result of my little lesson to them upon how far a good rifle in the hands of a French sergeant-major will carry. At least eighteen in all. I swear to you that I was shocked. It was a little too close to assassination.

John stared at me with his tarboosh jammed on his bushy gray eyebrows. He much resembled a well-fed owl. His beak was powerful, and he was of even thickness down to the point where his shanks appeared from his wide Turkish breeches. His brother, Boulos, I used to call the little owl. He had perhaps more sense, but lacked the dignity. Both of them were bound in decency to exclaim their amazement and felicitations; but I knew what they were thinking. In the eye of the mind they saw the blood money we should have to pay. One cannot massacre true believers in a Moslem country. It is not enough to say, as children do, that the other began it.

We decided to keep our mouths shut. The Christian Arab is accustomed to be discreet. He has the experience of twelve hundred years behind him. There was no reason at all to tell the truth to the other inhabitants of Ferjeyn, who only knew that I had been the first to venture out into the square and that I was armed. But that much was to be expected of a man who had been a soldier.

Helena had been listening from the next room. That is the custom, and very useful — for a silent audience always gets more sense out of a debate than the participants, who for half the time are not listening but thinking of what they will say next.

When the party had gone she asked me why I had fought. To my fellow townsmen that was no problem; they all liked to imagine themselves doing what I had done. But Helena was puzzled. Of course she was. During those weeks before the raid I had tried hard to make her understand that it was ridiculous for a man such as I to shout and wave a gun and run away with honor satisfied. And at last she had agreed that, if I would not do that, it was reasonable to keep out of local quarrels.

I could not attempt to explain to her that it was the stone which changed my mind. She would not have understood. Her home was sacred to her, but not the commune where she lived. Helena would have been quite content, provided she had her children and her husband, to inhabit a desert island.

I told her, therefore, that I had lost my temper. That was something wholly alien, but to which she was accustomed. I hasten to say, M. le Consul, that with my family I rarely lost my temper. But at inanimate objects — like, for example, an obstinate tree root in the field or the rusted split pin of an axle — it was my custom to curse like a madman. Such impatience is wholly European, so my outbreaks were a complete mystery to Helena. She took all as explained when I said that the stupidity of a Moslem fanatic affected me like an inanimate object. And it is possible that I was telling more truth than I knew.

In the evening a whole troop of gendarmerie rode clinking and stumbling up the track to Ferjeyn. They had come, they said, to protect us from the vengeance of the Moslems. That was mere courtesy. They knew as well as we did that those poor beggars down in the plain had had a bellyful that would last them for years. What they wanted was the truth, and they were going to stay with us until they got it.

They were good material. I could have used some of them

myself in old days. And they behaved decently. That was understandable, since we fed men and horses as if they had been our invited guests. The captain was an old gray fox in his fifties, with thirty years' experience of Syrian lies. We couldn't fool him and we did not try. Every man and woman said honestly where they had been during the raid, and of course their stories tallied. There was only one liar in Ferjeyn, and that was I. I told him the truth, too, up to a point — that I was not afraid of the Moslems since I had many friends among them, and that I had stayed at home and taken no part in the defense. My papers were in order, and he had no reason to doubt that I was indeed Nadim Nassar, who had spent twenty years in Morocco and France before returning home. My fellow townsmen did not talk of my origin; they were not asked. In any case I think they had all forgotten my real name. As for the Moslems of the plain, they only remembered that I had once been in the French Army — which was nothing extraordinary.

For a week the gendarmerie gave us no peace. We were always being visited by the sergeants, or summoned to the captain. They interrogated us separately and together, and confronted us with each other. As policemen, they were not bad at all. They had been trained by us, and some of them, during the war, worked with the British, too. But their task was hopeless. No one had seen the shots fired. Everyone could say where he was, and had witnesses.

Then the whole investigation was bedeviled by a message from the magistrate who had been taking depositions among the Moslems. They insisted that they had been fired on by a machine gun. It is probable that they believed it. In any case they could never admit that they had run in panic from a single rifle.

The captain started on the machine gun. It is not difficult for an experienced man to tell whether Arabs are lying or not. I do not say he will get the truth in the end; but he will know whether or not it is being told. The gendarmerie searched for that machine gun, and did more damage to our houses than the raiders. And all the time the captain watched our faces. At the end he could have no doubt there was no machine gun.

Then the old fool of a priest, who was not in the secret, suggested that perhaps a band of fellow Christians had heard of our danger and ridden three hundred miles from Anti-Lebanon to help us. I have more respect for the Church than my father had, but one must admit that they can never let well alone.

It was a most improbable suggestion. Such a thing was unheard of. And how could a band of Christians have crossed the plain and hidden themselves on our mountain without being seen? But the captain was so puzzled that he did not rule out this preposterous miracle. He searched the whole mountain, looking for the tracks of horses and the empties from the machine gun.

At last the gendarmerie left us. Horses and equipment in good order, they rode off down the hill. Considering that they had been five years without a French officer, they were well disciplined and a credit to their training. Nor did they lose interest in us. They chose their agents cleverly; during the next month there were several strangers who visited

Ferjeyn to buy or sell — all of them Christians, one a distant relative of the priest. But not another fact did they learn. I repeat: the whole village, except myself, had only to tell the truth.

Meanwhile the Moslems of the plain were overwhelmed by the consequences of their little outing. Not only had their losses been staggering for such a raid, but the government, having now sufficient excuse to arrest anyone it liked, made a clean sweep of all political opponents. The plain swarmed with police and troops. The Moslem headmen were not allowed to bargain with us or to threaten feud. It was evident that the affair was not going to be settled by our immemorial methods, but by administrative action as in Europe.

On the face of it this suited Ferjeyn. We should not have to kill half our sheep for a week's feasting while peace was made, or pay the ruinous blood money expected. But we were not altogether content. Red tape and good order were as unfamiliar to us as to the Moslems. And we did not like the silence of the authorities.

John and Boulos Douaihy went to see the provincial governor. They were very well received. He apologized to them for the lack of police protection, and assured them that the history of raids between Christian and Moslem was now closed forever. That was welcome, so far as it went. But John and his brother had the impression that they were being treated as the chiefs of a wild tribe. The governor was polite, but supercilious. And, what was worse, he appeared to believe the rumor that Ferjeyn had somehow received aid from a secret society of fellow Christians.

A month later the shock arrived. No fines, no punishment. A civilized solution. The inhabitants of Ferjeyn were to be moved right across Syria to the south of Damascus, and to take over a village of Moslems which was entirely surrounded by Christians. There would be an exchange of population as just as could be arranged, hectare for hectare and house for house. It was an act typical of the modern state. Any brutality is permissible if it simplifies the work of government servants — exception made, of course, of diplomats, M. le Consul, who maintain always the highest traditions.

Even then there was no question of handing me over. They were very loyal, my two owls. But I could not hesitate. Another man, less skeptical than I, might have spent a week of sleepless nights under the illusion that he had a decision to make. To me it was perfectly clear that what I feared had arrived, and that I could only obey my destiny.

I summoned the four notables of Ferjeyn who knew the truth, and told them that I would confess. They were astounded. I swear it had not yet occurred to them as a solution. My father-in-law and his friends were proud men, and it was not in accordance with their traditions to hand over a citizen of the commune to justice, even if he were a French deserter.

Well, but it was the obvious way out. And at last they agreed that I should tell the truth — on condition that a sure way of escape for me could be found. They promised to cherish Helena and the children, and to send me some of the proceeds of my land if it could possibly be done.

I noticed that John, though he exclaimed with the rest,

was not altogether sincere. I thought that perhaps he doubted whether my confession would put off the fate of Ferjeyn. I assured him that it would. I know the Syrian officials. Even when they are determined to be Western, they do not want more work than they can help. If they were certain that the slaughter at Ferjeyn was the work of one man and that the Christians, there and elsewhere, were just as tame as they had always been, all this exchange of population would be too much bother.

Yes, John agreed to all that. It was not the question which was troubling him. He took refuge in his owlishness, and said that we had discussed enough for the day, and he would tell us what he thought another time. The fact was that he did not wish to spoil an evening in which everyone had expressed such admirable and generous sentiments. In a French town he would have been a born chairman of committees.

We all insisted that he should speak out. He was the oldest of us and, when it came to local customs, by far the wisest.

"My son, Nadim Nassar, has killed forty men," he said — the total had become a little exaggerated. "We shall watch day and night. We shall turn ourselves into soldiers, and Ferjeyn into a camp. But even so we cannot be sure of protecting his children from revenge. The Moslems know how to wait. One year. Two years. And at last we shall find my grandchildren dead and mutilated."

It was true. I might escape or the government might imprison me. But in the end my boys would fall to the bullet and the knife.

"If only it were possible for us to swear by God that he was mad, and be believed!"

It was the saddler who thus regretted my sanity. But he was on to a good idea. There is no blood feud against the children of a madman.

To pretend to be a lunatic! M. le Consul, the more I thought of it, the more I liked it. And in that case the Moslems would no longer feel disgraced. They would be predisposed to accept the explanation. To run from a madman with a rifle — well, who wouldn't?

It was clear to me that one only needed a little cunning. I have no faith in plans, which are always worthless, but when it comes to putting on a comedy I am in my element. Any experienced sergeant-major has acquired a sense of stage management.

I told the four to keep silent about my intentions, and that in a day or two I would have something to propose. At work and in the silence of the night I rehearsed the scene in my imagination, and when I had convinced myself that it would succeed, I talked to Helena. She was appalled when I told her that to save our little town I had determined to confess. Since Ferjeyn had not demanded the sacrifice, she saw no necessity for it at all. She was quite ready to exchange her house for some filthy Moslem hovel. When she had cleaned it for a month, she insisted, we should not know the difference.

And then she relieved herself with tears. She could not sleep, she told me — myself, I am always drowned in sleep — for terror of what might happen to the boys if ever it became known to the Moslems that I alone had been responsible for so many deaths. I think it was she who put the idea into the head of her father.

She claimed the right of wife and children to go with me, if I must confess and escape. But that was impossible. She had no conception of the life of an outlaw. To cross, all of us, into Turkey or Iraq was easy. And what then? A man accompanied by his family must have open dealings with strangers and foreign police. I was a French deserter. I could not account for myself — unless I gave my identity as Nadim Nassar of Ferjeyn. And if I did that, we should never have an hour when we could feel safe.

No. Alone I could vanish and perhaps remake a life. Meanwhile she would be living in comfort on her own land with her father to protect her.

Then I explained to her how I meant to save the children from blood feud. She was wise in the ways of her country, and she agreed that my scheme was possible. But not in one single detail must it fail. Raving and clowning, she said, would not be enough. To convince my public I must commit some horror that no Arab — if he were only pretending to be mad — would ever dream of. And that was to shoot her.

We were a model couple. The wives of Ferjeyn would hold me up to their husbands as a paragon. That was easier for them than to try to imitate Helena. If I could have brought myself to do so, I would have beaten her once or twice just to make the lives of my friends more peaceful. Even the Moslems spoke of Nadim Nassar and his wife. And so, if I were seen to aim at her and shoot, there would be no doubt that I was mad.

She insisted. She had no fear. She thought that a soldier such as I could pick his target and, even in a moment of emotion, separate one toe from the rest. But she knew her people. There does not exist an Arab — unless trained by Europeans — who could aim at his wife and be sure of not hitting her. For them it would be an act of homicidal lunacy impossible to feign.

It was only the four notables of Ferjeyn whom I let into the secret. The rest of my fellow townsmen continued to be left in ignorance. John Douaihy was certain that they too would be convinced I was mad. He had no fear for his daughter. It is extraordinary how the Arabs, who are always letting off firearms, never trouble to find out what is practical and what is not.

We sent messengers to the headmen of the villages in the plain. Nothing was said of peacemaking and compensation. We hinted — in a courteous tone of regret for old times — that the government would not allow us to take the initiative. All we wanted was an informal meeting to settle up our business affairs with old Moslem friends. We said, too — to tempt their avarice — that we might be selling some land and stock before the exchange of population.

The notables of the plain sent us back an answer which was reasonably cordial, for none of them wanted us to be removed from our mountain. An interest would be gone from their empty lives. Besides, they preferred people they knew to people they did not, whatever their religion.

The day fixed for the meeting was very hot. That's understood, of course. But it was an afternoon when even the rock lizards sought the shade. The plain was indistinguish-

able from a desert, and on the mountain the dust rose in
eddies from our terraces and reddened the leaves of the
orchards. Eight of the notables came, with their principal
relations and retainers. After talks (which had no content
but politeness) the cushions and carpets were spread under
the pillars of the square, and some thirty of us, who were
the most important, sat down to eat. The women served us.
Helena had put on her native costume. She was like the girls
of the Crusaders, flowing in robes and embroidery. There
was certainly plenty to hit without touching flesh.

It was more dignified than gay, our feast. Naturally there
was still some reserve. But manners were effortless since
our customs were the same. Sometimes it seems to me a
pity that the Arabs ever divided themselves into Christians
and Moslems. They should have remained idolaters like the
Hindus.

I had hidden my rifle on a rooftop across the square. None
of us carried arms beyond those for pure decoration. Between John and me was sitting an old fool of a sheik, a
man of the utmost stupidity and kindliness. He resembled
French generals I have known. He was so harmless that it
was incredible anyone should outrage his feelings. A great
dish of rice was placed in front of him. At that moment I
seized him by the back of the neck and plunged his face
and beard in it. For good measure I emptied the cream
salad over my father-in-law. Then shouting and laughing I
leaped over the heads of those who sat opposite me on the
ground, and lost myself in the alleys on the other side of
the square.

When I reappeared upon the roof they had not recovered from their surprise. John Douaihy was screaming apologies, and swearing that I was more Frenchman than Syrian and that I had lost my wits in the sun like any dog of a European. Bareheaded and clothes torn, I capered upon the rooftop, firing shots. The Moslems were in panic. It was an unmistakable echo of the night of the raid. I think it had occurred to them, minutes before my friends took oath on it, that I might have been their only serious enemy.

I began to curse Ferjeyn and the wife who had brought me there, and I shot in the general direction of Helena. It was not difficult to miss her, but to appear mad and to miss all the other women too — well, I doubt if that scene alone would have been convincing. But Helena acted magnificently. She ran like a terrified chicken. And then, according to our arrangement, she stood still in the middle of the square and raised her arms to me for mercy.

It was a moment more tense than any crisis of war. I forced myself to concentrate. I found afterwards that my teeth had bitten deep into my tongue. I fired. She fell like a dead woman. I shall never forget how the cries of the people in the square were all at once silenced. I watched her face, which they could not see, and she made me a little smile of congratulation. Another second, and I should have blown my brains out.

She told me, when I saw her again, that the bullet had passed through the great wings of her arms as she lifted them, and close to the body. And then what did she do, my well-beloved? She passed her left hand under her robe and ripped the flesh from a rib with the nail of her middle finger so that it would appear she had been grazed.

That will seem to you barbarous, M. le Consul, but it was for her children.

They chased me, but not too close — for John and Boulos deliberately led the pursuit up the wrong alley. Meanwhile, I dropped to the ground in front of the saddler's shop. He had left his stable open, as if by accident, and his horse saddled. A pretty price he charged for it, too. But he had the right, and one must not ask too much of one's friends.

I rode through the olives and up across my own land by a little path, where no one who did not know every stone of it would dare to follow at the gallop. There were several shots fired after me — perhaps by our guests, perhaps by men of Ferjeyn who were horrified as much by the breach of hospitality as by my treatment of Helena. I passed my house and waved to my boys. Their dear faces were full of conflict as those of men. They were wildly excited by my speed, but they could not help knowing that the bullets which cut the leaves and whined were meant for me.

By God, when it was all over, I think my four friends themselves were mystified! There had been, I must admit, a certain gusto in my acting — in all, that is, that did not concern Helena. It was a relief, for once, to be permitted to have the manners of an apache and push a venerable beard into the eternal rice. There is no doubt, M. le Consul, that in the long run it is a strain for us to behave as formally as Arabs. I am ashamed of it, but I cannot deny it.

All the night I rode east towards the frontier, skirting the foothills of the Jebel Sinjar. The western end of the

range is in Syria, and at the tip of it is the isolated mountain on which stands Ferjeyn; the eastern end is in Iraq.
I had no idea what would happen or what pursuit there
would be. The only certainty was that the notables of Ferjeyn would inform the authorities, and that the gendarmerie
would be on the lookout for a madman with a rifle. I laid a
trail that they could follow into Iraq.

On the second night I traveled north along the frontier
and crossed back again into Syria. Then I rode north for a
third night and forded the Tigris. Once over the river, a
fugitive has only to follow the tangle of tributaries up into
the hills. He is in country as green and wild as the Auvergne,
but far less inhabited. And there is nothing but the uniform
of the frontier patrols to tell him whether he is in Iraq or
Turkey.

The little money that I had was enough for my necessities. I slept on the ground — which is no hardship in Au-
gust — and I bought my bread in the villages, telling lies
to account for myself. Up there one does not ask questions
of a man with a rifle if he can pay his way.

But a rifle is more valuable than any gold. If you are to
keep it, you must sleep on it. When I was in Weygand's
Army of the Orient, I remember that at night we chained
our rifles to the tent pole. Well, there were eight weary men
sleeping in a tent. A clever Arab chief loosened the guy
ropes and lifted the pole without waking one of them. In
the morning there was not a rifle among the lot.

I tell you this story, M. le Consul, that you may not
think too hardly of me, a sergeant-major, for nearly losing
my own. I was sleeping under the trees at the bend of a

stream. Unlike the fast water on my land, it made a noise, that stream. It was impatient for the Tigris and the Persian Gulf. I surrendered myself utterly to the grass that was my bed. I was not overweary, but I longed for Ferjeyn and Helena and my boys. When one is unhappy one takes refuge in sleep as in a drug.

He had taken my rifle from under my body without waking me, but at the last moment the trigger guard caught on the buckle of my bandolier. I was festooned with cartridges like some damned Russian dancer in a cabaret. He pulled and ran for it, but I, I was only five yards behind. When he stopped to fire at me from the hip I dived under the barrel and drove home my knife in his stomach.

I am no Good Samaritan, I assure you. But it grieved me to kill an honest man who was only stealing a rifle. I might have done the same, if I had had the skill.

"When did you eat last?" I asked him.

My interest was technical. If there was anything in his stomach, he was a dead man.

"The day before yesterday," he answered.

"God is Great, brother!" I said to him, and put him on my horse with his headcloth wrapped round his guts.

We were, I think, in Turkey, but the nearest town where there would be a doctor was Zakho in Iraq. It was not far — about thirty kilometers. And I knew the track. He was all skin and muscle like a dried herring. The stomach of the very poor is tough. I told him that if he would oblige me by keeping alive till morning we might save him yet.

We talked a little on the way. He was a Yezidi from the eastern end of the Jebel Sinjar, and he knew Ferjeyn. The

Moslems hate the Yezidis even more than Christians, but have no fear of them. They are few, and do not put up any competition. Devil worshipers they are called, because they think it tactful to be just as polite to the powers of evil as those of good. That seems to me very reasonable.

Times were hard in the Jebel Sinjar. The Iraqi end of the range is not so fertile as our little Syrian tip. So my Yezidi was going to live with his brother, who had a permit to cut and sell timber on the frontier. He had not wished to arrive empty-handed.

M. le Consul, I must apologize for all these details. You cannot be interested in the banal stories of criminals, which are not in essence very different whether they take place at the Porte de Vincennes or the headwaters of the Tigris. But I wish to show you the sort of people among whom I lived. They being what they are and I being an outlaw, my conduct becomes explicable.

There was a sort of doctor in Zakho, for the English had established a clinic there. The idea, I think, was public hygiene. But the people of Zakho are far more concerned with the cure of wounds. It's experience that counts. Me, if I had a hole in my belly, I'd rather be patched up at the regimental aid post than the finest hospital in Paris.

Well, whether it was the Iraqi doctor or a grateful devil, my Yezidi did not die. I remained in the neighborhood. I had nothing to do, and to visit the sickbed became an occupation. I met Merjan, the timber cutter. He was a man of magnificent mustaches, dressed in rags but well armed. He told me that if his brother did not recover, he would send me to hell to be the dead man's servant; and if he lived, then all of his clan would be my friends forever. It was hardly logical, but those chaps are composed of nothing but emotion.

When the man was up, with no more entrances to his stomach than the good Lord provided, I went to work with the brothers. As I had suspected from Merjan's heroics, timber cutting was not his only occupation. It is incredible, the life between Lake Van and the frontiers. Into those remote hills the law penetrates so seldom that the tribesmen in their spare time are amateur cattle thieves and smugglers, and even professional criminals can sow and gather a crop before they have to move on. Merjan, under cover of his wood cutting, was a sort of Thomas Cook for brigands. He was guide, intermediary and warehouseman.

I had little to do with all that. It was I who cut the wood, with two half-wit Turks to help me. I was allowed to make a living. I sold my horse to buy better tools, and often I had more cash in my belt than Merjan and his brother. The district is so poor and so wild that even by breaking the law there is little money to be gained.

M. le Consul, I am not naturally an outlaw. I cannot live away from my fellows; perhaps it is because my father was so long mayor of his town. I began to make the disastrous habit of going down to Zakho once or twice a week when the day's work was over. It was not so handsome a village as Ferjeyn, but more European, with shops of a sort and good paved streets. The landscape was not that of Syria and Iraq. There were willows and poplars everywhere, and meadows by the river that were green even in September. I dreamed of bringing Helena and my boys to Zakho, for

I had begun to feel at ease across the Tigris. I had forgotten that to Arabs a line drawn on the map is of no importance. For us, to cross a frontier is to be safe; for them, a frontier is merely a God-sent convenience for making money.

I sat at the entrance to a wineshop, talking with two friends. When business was over, Zakho was a silent little town. A footfall, the murmur of the streams, the low voices of women behind shutters and courtyard doors — those were all one heard. I did not expect the harsh voice of an Arab, calling me by the name of Nadim Nassar.

I looked up. It was a certain Zeid, a dealer in sheep and mangy camels — a wild-eyed barbarian who knew no law but what he misconceived to be his religion. I had seen him in the square of Ferjeyn, with foam on his villainous mouth and an old sword that had been used on women. I had unfortunately missed my shot at him. He was regarding Zakho with disgust, for it was a town of heretics: Yezidis, Shias, Kurds, Alaouites — let alone Christians and a few Jews.

"You do not appear very mad, Nadim Nassar," he said.

"My mind has cleared, thanks be to God," I answered, and my friends stared — for it was a pleasant bit of scandal that my name was Nassar and I had been mad.

"It has cleared very quickly. God is indeed Great," Zeid replied.

M. le Consul, there was irony in his voice that would have befitted a university professor — except that it lacked subtlety.

I hailed him as an old friend and took him by the hand

and asked him where he meant to spend the night. The idiot was so full of contempt that he thought I was afraid. I left my friends and led him round the corner into a street where, I said, there was good coffee. He went with me, continuing to give thanks for my deliverance. His poor brain was pleased with the simple jest. He could not have told me more plainly what he meant to do on his return to his village. There was no one in the street, and it was nearly dark. I killed him quickly and mercifully, and laid his body behind a pile of dung and rubbish.

It was hardly the act of a respectable Frenchman. But what else could I do? Was Zeid to be allowed to return home and scream that Nadim Nassar had been pretending madness? He was just the type to conceal himself among Helena's olives with his rusty sword.

Beyond Zakho, it is true, there was a convenient lack of law and order, but in the town itself were more or less civilized police. I had to be far away before Zeid's body was discovered. Merjan, by good fortune, was at our timber camp. I told him what had happened. It was unnecessary to give details. I had only to sketch the character of Zeid, and explain that there was a blood feud between us.

The Yezidis meet with so few friends that they give absolute loyalty to those they have. Merjan on the instant took food, water and arms, and marched me off through the hills to seek a party of his clients from whom we could borrow ponies. Before dawn we had crossed into Syria. The next night we rode south, parallel to the frontier — it was routine, that — and crossed back again into Iraq. By the third dawn we were among the rocks of the Jebel Sinjar, and exchanging shouts with Merjan's own people.

"Go where you will, freely," Merjan said to me. "And if you wish to visit Ferjeyn, you shall be passed from friend to friend as far as the last village of Yezidis, who will guide you across the frontier and receive you on your return."

He left me with his parents, and rode back to Zakho with the ponies. I stayed at his father's house as long as politeness demanded, and then begged to be sent on to the western end of the Jebel. To my regret I saw none of the rites of their religion. The devil does no better or worse for them than for other mountain Arabs. They are hospitable, kindly and very poor. In the heat of their rocks there is a fine foretaste of hell — but if in the East one belongs to a sect that is hated it is as well to find an inaccessible home.

From village to village I was passed along the upper slopes of the range into Syria. There, in the no man's land, I was still a long day's march from my home, but the plain below me to the north was the same that for eight years I had seen from the heights above Ferjeyn.

The Jebel between Ferjeyn and the frontier was worthless and eroded country, inhabited only by a few miserable goatherds. I passed through it cautiously, seen only from a distance and, since I was armed, avoided. At dusk I arrived on the pastures above Ferjeyn. I was so excited that I could have embraced the nearest cow. But I contained myself. There were two horses grazing. They looked to me like gendarmerie horses. I was sure they belonged to no one in the commune.

When it was dark I dropped from terrace to terrace and down the beds of streams. It was better not to take the path until I knew more about those horses. There was a light in my house behind the shutters, and I heard the voice of Helena singing to the children. I knelt in the shadows below the window and called softly to her. Her voice ceased. She thought it was only her singing which had summoned me. Then I called again, and she opened for me a window in a room that was dark.

M. le Consul, I do not know if you are happily married, with a family. If you are not, and I should describe my feelings, you would accuse me of exaggeration. If you are, I have no need to explain. In any case, imagine that for two months you have lived my life and have had no chance to send or receive a message. We were all wet with tears. I think I have made it clear that we were a singularly united family.

Helena told me that Ferjeyn was watched. It was said that Nadim Nassar had killed again in Zakho, and that he had taken refuge in the Jebel Sinjar. The Yezidis had sworn that they knew nothing of me, but Merjan had been seen returning north to the Tigris, and leading a saddled pony. Ferjeyn was terrified lest I should cross the Jebel and return. John Douaihy had not dared — in case some fool should talk — to tell them that I had only pretended to be mad.

I calmed Helena. I was not going to lose the joy of homecoming for the sake of worrying about what might never happen. A family is much like a squadron. The last man to show fear must be the sergeant-major. We closed

down the shutters and made a feast. The harvest, thank
God, had been good, and Helena was not in want. She had
even set by a small store of money for me. And so the little
family jokes were repeated, and we laughed at them as
though I had never been away. At last the children slept
where they sat, and we put them to bed.

In the morning it was a question where to hide. We did
not live in luxury. There were four whitewashed rooms in
my house, all opening out of the little guest hall. The
furniture would not have concealed a frightened rabbit, and
anyone passing could look in through the windows.

Helena went up to the flat roof and reported that there
were men of Ferjeyn on the terraces and the path, and
that those who were working their fields were armed. It
was idiotic that they should be afraid of me. But all the
poor fools knew was that on my last appearance I had tried
to kill my wife.

The children went to school. It was not necessary to tell
them to say nothing; we warned them, however, not to
show their excitement by a single look or word among themselves. Yes, M. le Consul, the priest has a sort of school
at Ferjeyn. He teaches them to read and write Arabic, and
such history as he knows. It is naturally somewhat special-
ized. They can read French, too, for I taught them myself.
And I have always spoken French with them as much as
Arabic. M. le Consul, I beg of you — take them when the
time comes. They are fine youngsters, and they will be valuable to France.

I had thought of going out to the barn and making myself vanish among the fodder; but it was impossible to get

there without being seen. Well, I am an old campaigner and I had need of sleep. What better than to take it, hiding under the bed? Sometimes I heard callers, and once Helena led a woman into the room and sat talking, being careful to wake me up lest I should snore. I did not care. I fell asleep again. The floor of my own home caressed my body.

Then John Douaihy arrived. Helena led him to our room so that I might know who had come and that he was unaccompanied. I assure you that he was telling Helena she should not remain alone in the house.

"God grant you more brains in your fat head, O my father!" I said to him from under the bed.

I could only see him from feet to knees. They trembled like those of a Syrian dancing girl. I poked out my head and told him not to be a fool.

"But you killed Zeid," he stammered.

They are a feminine folk, the Arabs. After a while they are taken in by their own lies. By now John Douaihy himself had begun to believe I might be mad — it is possible that he had not forgiven me the salad — and if Helena had not laughed at him I think he would have backed out of the room. To be giggled over by a daughter — there's nothing like that for bringing a man back to common sense.

Yes, I had killed Zeid, and I told him why. He had only time to lean down — for I was still under the bed — and take my hand between his and promise to tell his people that it was shameful to hunt a citizen of Ferjeyn, whether mad or not, and that they must not shoot so long as my rifle was slung. And then the gendarmerie were at the door.

There were two of them. They came with the news that I

must be lying up close to or on our mountain. The goatherds
of the Jebel Sinjar had seen a man with a rifle hiding
among the rocks at dusk and looking down into the saddle
between the main range and the hill of the Christians. It
was true that for a few minutes I had been careless. But the
first sight of Ferjeyn pastures was full of emotion.

All the doors from the guest hall were open. In so fresh
and empty and wind-swept a house the gendarmes could see
at once I was not there. And both Helena and her father
were calm. John Douaihy, from the moment of the knock
on the door, had become the dignified headman of his commune. In spite of his appearance, the old owl could surrender himself to his feelings like a child. During a mere
five minutes he had been overcome by the demands of terror, of affection, and now of duty. He led the gendarmes
away. As a father-in-law he was worth many more civilized.
I should like to hold his hand again.

I was encircled, M. le Consul. And no means of breaking
through. Two Syrian troopers were not much of a force
against a sergeant-major, but what about my fellow townsmen and, beyond them, the Moslems of the plain? I had no
wish to start a battle with either. It looked as if I had only
two alternatives: to give myself up or to remain in the house
until the search for me slackened. But the latter was impossible. The oldest of my boys was only seven. At that age
children can act a part for a few hours, but not day after
day.

The tactical position was simple enough even for a gendarme. There were a dozen routes by which I could leave
my house, but if I went up I must somewhere cross the

pastures on top of the hill; and if I went down I must go through Ferjeyn. So I knew more or less where the pickets would be. True, they were expecting my arrival, whereas I was trying to get away. But that made no difference.

I asked Helena to go out at dusk and try to report to me where the gendarmes were and what the organization of the people of Ferjeyn was. All the same, I had not much confidence. She would be closely watched for her own safety, or because it might be thought that she was trying to find me.

"That is what I should do!" she cried. "Nothing could keep me from going to find my husband."

"But he is difficult to find," I laughed. "Since he ran away from you, he has learned too much from bad characters."

"You would send me a message," she said.

Well, there, out of our pleasantries, leaped the scheme. It was ready-made. It only needed details to be filled in by a woman's wit and a soldier's experience.

A basket of food to be left out for me. Excellent! Where to leave it? But the answer springs to the lips. Where there was a clear field of fire, so that the gendarmes could settle down on a rock overlooking the basket, and be confident. Then the men of Ferjeyn had to be considered. They must be decoyed away from the route I would take back to the Jebel Sinjar.

It was easy. There was a little glade on the southwestern slope of the mountain, commanded by the necessary rock. It was a spot well known to us, where we used to go in the heat of summer, before the babies could walk, and let them

crawl on the grass. Now, if I were coming from the Jebel
I should traverse the southern slopes of our mountain and
reach that glade without ever crossing the pastures. And any
man of Ferjeyn would be sure of it. So there was no need
for any cordon across the top.

Helena made up a basket of food, and pretended to be
taking it up the mountain to her uncle. Boulos was really
there, hoping, I am sure, to warn me off if he could; it was
not likely that John would have had a chance to speak with
him yet. First, she had to find the gendarmes and act suspiciously and draw their attention. Then she must make
them follow her, and pretend not to be aware of it. That
was difficult — impossible if she had not been acting in
character. But all Ferjeyn knew what she was. If a starving
husband had managed to let her know he needed food, she
would have blindly taken it to him, though he were armed
and mad and had tried to kill her.

She returned at the beginning of the night. Meanwhile
the children had come home and were keeping guard —
all but the youngest, who was under the bed with me.
She had no doubt that she had been followed. The
gendarme was clumsy when sneaking through the woods
on foot.

I said my farewells, and plunged into a night that was
also of the spirit. As I have said, I planned to go back to the
Yezidis. The route, the people, the hiding places, I had
worked them all out. A lot of fuss about nothing. Such plan-
ning was against my principles. I should have known better.

On the track between my house and the pastures there

should be a picket. Even if I were expected elsewhere, that was an elementary precaution to take for the safety of my wife and children. I was glad to find three of my fellow townsmen alert and in the position I would have chosen for them myself. It gave me confidence that Helena was always in their thoughts. With all its faults, it was a gallant little town, my Ferjeyn. The three men were facing uphill, and I was able to leave the track and pass boldly round them. When they heard me, they challenged. I replied in the falsetto of an idiot that it was Nadim Nassar returning from his wife. They laughed.

It was impossible to guess the position of the rest. If the men of Ferjeyn wished to capture me before I collected my basket of food, they would be under cover on the eastern slope; if they wanted the gendarmes to take all responsibility, they would be in the trees between the glade and my house, ready to pick up my body or intercept me if I escaped. In either case they would not be on the pastures.

As in all attempts to predict the behavior of opponents, my reasoning was neither right nor wrong. There were, in fact, a few men on the top; but they kept to the east, well away from the gendarmes' preserves. The pasture was by no means an open alp. It was the rugged top of a mountain, sown with rocks and bushes, where the grass grew in hundreds of little patches rather than a continuous meadow. Well, with the half-moon showing every bush as a movement and every shadow as inhabited, the men of Ferjeyn were nervous. They were smoking, and whispering to keep up their courage. They were not much use as soldiers. The cattle were in more danger than I.

Without difficulty I reached the little cliff which overlooked our glade. The basket was half concealed under a bush. Since I knew where to look for it, I could just distinguish the white cloth. The two gendarmes I could not see, but I knew exactly where they were — flat on their rumbling bellies under the overhang of the cliff with their carbines trained on the basket.

Their horses were tethered on the pasture, behind a rock. As soon as I found them I saw my opportunity. Good Lord, how right I had been to feel skeptical of my plans for returning to the Jebel Sinjar!

I inserted a prickly burr under the tail of one of those patient animals. He did not like that at all. You would have said, a charging elephant! One gendarme came up to see what was wrong. He was so much occupied with the horse that I was able to measure my blow. It was enough to leave him breathing quietly on the ground.

He could not answer inquiries himself and I did not know him well enough to imitate his voice, so I only had time to change into half his uniform when the other gendarme, alarmed at the silence, advanced to see what had happened. He caught me at a disadvantage. I had his comrade's breeches round my ankles. I should have shot quickly. But, M. le Consul, I did not wish to become, like John Douaihy, frightened of myself. I pretended to be demoralized, to beg for mercy. And he, thinking of the boasting he could enjoy if he took Nadim Nassar singlehanded, came too close to use his arms. Since he struck me twice across the face, I was not so gentle with him as with the other.

I left them well tied up with the spare reins and halter,

confident that they would not be found till morning. And there! I had a horse to ride, another to lead, two carbines and two pistols as well as my own rifle. I trotted across the pasture and down the track, past the picket, past my house and through the streets of Ferjeyn. On my head I carried the spare saddle to conceal my face. I gave the impression of an extremely angry gendarme in a hurry, and answered questions only with muttered curses.

There was neither telephone nor telegraph in Ferjeyn. By riding hard due north across the Duck's Bill, I reckoned to be over the Turkish frontier before the alarm had gone out. They were two fresh horses and I did not spare them. In the morning, galloping through Moslem villages where they tried to stop me to hear why I was riding so fast, I may have aroused some suspicion. But once near the frontier I had no more trouble. It cannot have been an uncommon sight — a silent gendarme in a hurry, leading the horse of his dead comrade.

And then I made a circuit through the Turkish hills — not so easy, M. le Consul, that it can be dismissed in a sentence, but I am conscious that I may have kept you too long from more important work — and I descended cautiously upon the camp of Merjan.

It is a refuge, that country, and beautiful, but miserably poor. Three rifles, two pistols, their ammunition and two horses was a considerable capital. Merjan decided that he and his brother and I could live more freely than as timber cutters and middlemen for smugglers. With a Russian deserter, a Turk and a Persian — of true officer material, but having felt it his duty to assassinate a political — we formed a band. I should not like you to think that we are criminals on a European scale. In the first place there is practically nothing here worth stealing. But we can go where we wish without interference, and we are on good terms with the tribes. In return for food, we give them protection from police and bandits. And if they do not wish for protection we make it desirable. Sometimes, too, we act as escort for smugglers. In fact one does what one can. But it is not a life for a man who loves to be in his own town.

M. le Consul, for myself I have no right to ask more than what I have. I live, and when I die, there will be no fuss — unless Merjan and his brother devoutly say a prayer for me to the devil. But for my boys I beg your patronage and, through you, that of the Republic. I have no address, and Damascus is very far. Perhaps in the spring I shall be able to send another messenger to call on you. Perhaps he will bring back to me a word of comfort.

Awaiting your reply, I beg you to accept, M. le Consul, the assurance of my highest consideration.

VALENTIN LECORMIER

Annex to the Statement of Sergeant-major Lecormier

QUAI D'ORSAY
20TH APRIL, 1952

DEAR CONSUL AND OLD COMRADE,

But what a document! It is not often in these days that we get anything from our representatives abroad to entertain us. You have the thanks of the whole department.

He's a type, your bandit! As I look at it, only once in his life has he made a wrong decision, and that upset him so badly that he denies we can ever make decisions at all. You really must do something for him. As a bureaucrat, one gets so bored with being inhuman.

Here is the minute I have received from the Ministry of War:

Lecormier, Valentin. Three times mentioned. Croix de Guerre. Missing in Cyprus 1944. Believed killed in interallied brawl, or suffering from loss of memory. Character excellent. An outstanding leader of men, whether native or metropolitan.

From discreet inquiries I learn that the major whom Lecormier crowned with a bottle — he now has his division — swore that they had both been attacked by drunken British. No one was more unhappy than he when Lecormier vanished, and it was he who suggested loss of memory.

Look, old man — that plea will be accepted. Lecormier, so far as France is concerned, has nothing whatever against his name. And we have urgent need of such old soldiers. We will find means of paying a passage to Marseille for his thirteenth-century Helena and the boys. As for him, you who are wise in the ways of the Orient can no doubt extract him, metamorphosed into a good French bourgeois, from his spider's web of frontiers. If he hesitates you may assure him that we know the taste of old warrant officers for garrison life, and that they are invariably stationed in a little town.

(Signature illegible)

Kindly Stranger

IT IS an odd thought — at this date, unworldly rather than disturbing — that I am responsible for all the disasters of the last forty years, for 1914-18, for the Russian Revolution, for Hitler. No Martian arriving from outer space could have changed the quietly running world into so devastatingly wrong and fast a gear. And, as in a cautionary tale for children, it all came about through disobedience.

My father had a dear friend named von Lech who was an undersecretary in the Austro-Hungarian Ministry of Education. They had really little in common except the self-confident liberalism of their time and a passionate interest in the art of teaching. Both of them believed that when all Europeans — the rest of the world could follow later — attended secondary school Utopia would have arrived. That did not seem so comical a creed in 1914 as it does now. It was a bond of idealism strong enough for them to visit each other, and even for their wives to be polite to each other.

Von Lech was a hard-working administrator who kept two servants, but no car or carriage. That was just the position of my father. Both of them could live comfortably and precisely in that state to which Emperor and King had called them, but holidays were always a minor problem and illness a major one.

Thus it was natural that when von Lech discovered a very cheap and hospitable hotel at Ilidza, an unknown summer resort in Austrian Bosnia, he should write to my father about it. He knew that my father was convalescing after a long illness and had been ordered by his doctor to go abroad for a rest. Frau von Lech also wrote to my mother in formal, diplomatic French. I think it was the use of French rather than German or English which overcame her mistrust. Ilidza was made to sound fashionable, which it wasn't, and romantic, which it was.

Neither of my parents knew anything whatever about Bosnia. My father, however, always accepted authority. Von Lech, it was plain, counted Bosnia a normal province of the Austro-Hungarian Empire. Provinces of the Empire were civilized and disciplined. It would therefore be an unwarranted misuse of the imagination to consider a visit to Ilidza at all adventurous. They decided to start in the middle of June. They would not hear of me traveling out by myself at the end of term — rightly, for at thirteen I was absurdly helpless — so I was let out of school six weeks early, and accompanied them by train to Trieste and by boat down the Adriatic.

Ilidza was intensely excited by the coming visit of the Archduke Francis Ferdinand and his pretty wife Sophie, Duchess of Hohenberg. I cannot remember if she was really pretty. Even to a sophisticated eye all feminine royalty is dazzling. But I can see the Archduke now. I was immensely impressed by him. Not only was he going to become an emperor, but he reminded me of a taller, fiercer and unsmiling edition of my headmaster.

The pair of them stayed at Ilidza for three nights while the Archduke attended the maneuvers. On June 28 they were to make a state visit to the neighboring town of Sarajevo; and the von Lechs, who highly approved of the solid glimmerings of liberalism in the Archduke, loyally determined to go over and cheer. Of course we went with them.

We watched from a first-floor balcony on the Appel Quay. The house was some fifty yards from the crossroads formed by Franz Josef Street and the Latin Bridge, and belonged to some hotel acquaintance of the von Lechs — an old lady in black who entertained us with little cakes, and wine in colored glasses. I think she must have been of rather lower social status, perhaps a native Bosnian, but I remember little about her except the colored glasses.

The Appel Quay was a long, straight road, bordered on one side by houses and on the other by the river. It was Sunday, and so there was a thick hedge of public on each side of the route. In the distance, to the right of our balcony, the procession was coming up the quay towards us when we heard a sharp explosion. The cars stopped. Hedges wavered inwards and were held back.

The women of our party screamed that it was a bomb. My mother watched Frau von Lech to see whether it would be proper to faint. Frau von Lech, however, decided that my mother would show the famous English phlegm and determined to imitate her. The old lady prayed, and fascinated me by the complicated gestures with which she crossed herself.

The men exerted their common-sense influence. Von Lech, who was still unused to cars, suggested that the noise had been due to a burst tire or petrol tank. My father said that the public should not be allowed to purchase fireworks. The bomb as a political weapon was inconceivable to such believers in Progress; they easily assumed that — except in Russia — it was inconceivable to everyone else.

I myself, with the superiority of a sound preparatory school, accepted their unimaginative confidence that the incident was trivial. The melancholy procession — now of three cars instead of four — restarted and passed hurriedly below our decorated balcony. The cheering was so thin that you could distinguish individual voices. I was disappointed. It seemed hardly worth the short journey from Ilidza for so small and dull an affair. My only comparable experience had been a visit of Edward VII to Gloucester. There had been lots of yeomanry in gorgeous uniforms. The genial, top-hatted figure in the open landau had created, by the mere force of his expansive masculinity, an air of festival.

But now that the Archduke had passed, we could see the missing fourth car drawn into the side of the road. A crowd, at a respectful distance, was round it. Another and more active crowd, led by police, was running up the dry bed of the river. We saw an indistinguishable limp puppet caught and arrested.

Von Lech, allowing a decent interval for the stopped clock of civilization to start again, leaned over the balcony and made inquiries. Yes, it had been a bomb; a colonel in the last car had been wounded; some Bosnian students were, it was believed, responsible. Von Lech and my father took this awkward hurdle in their stride. Secondary education, they admitted, was bound to have its teething troubles.

I was silent with a new disappointment. One read of bombs in the newspapers. Anarchists with bombs occasionally blew themselves up (but no one else) in the *Boys Own Paper*. And now a bomb had been thrown practically in front of my eyes, and I hadn't even seen it.

The party returned inside for refreshments. The women were exclamatory. My father and von Lech discussed bombs with philosophic detachment. Nobody paid any attention to me. I made myself a nuisance, and was told that I could go into the garden and look at the goldfish until the Archduke's procession returned along the quay, but that on no account was I to leave the house.

In cold blood I should never have dared to engage myself in the streets of so very foreign a town; but curiosity about the bomb overcame all else. I was as eager to get the horrid details for my school friends as any reporter for his editor. I quietly opened and closed the front door, and slunk along the Appel Quay, keeping close under the houses in case anyone should come out on the balcony and spot me. I crossed Franz Josef Street and then, with enough people between me and the balcony, went over to the river side of the quay.

There was nothing much to see at the car. The right back wheel and its mudguard looked as if they had been involved in a nasty smash — a sight far more familiar now than then. Imagination produced a few drops of blood on the road. Or perhaps they were really there.

I wandered along the embankment with some vague idea of detecting traces of the would-be assassin in the river bed. There were none, and I found myself quarter of a mile from home with no satisfactory reason for being where I was. I became embarrassedly conscious of my outlandish appearance. In honor of the Archduke I had been compelled to put on my Eton suit — then worn by all small boys on Sundays and formal occasions. I don't know whether Sarajevo had ever seen such an outfit before. No one assumed that I had escaped from a circus, so it cannot have been as startling as I supposed.

While I fiddled around, no doubt taking refuge in daydreams, the two hedges of police and public opposite our balcony had grown up again. The Archduke was due to return. Worse still, there was a third hedge stretching across the Appel Quay where the procession was to turn right into Franz Josef Street. I was completely cut off from home.

I disliked crossing the empty, wide road with everyone's eyes upon me. However, I had to get back to the balcony before my absence was discovered. I pushed self-consciously through the line of people into the open, and was at once turned back by a policeman. His reaction, I think, must have been one of sheer surprise. He was understandably nervous.

Turned back almost simultaneously was another spectator, a sharp-featured young man little taller than my overgrown self. He too was trying to cross the road and had left it too late. We exchanged glances. I remember his brilliant blue eyes in a yellowish face. He beckoned to me, and said in German (which I understood, though nothing would induce me to mumble it unless compelled):

"Come with me! I will take you across."

Then he asked the policeman if he couldn't see that I was a little well-born foreigner and harmless. His tone almost implied that he was my manservant or tutor. With an arm round my shoulders, taking away by his middle-class poverty the shame of my resplendent Eton suit, he led me across the road.

We entered the crowd lining the corner of the Appel Quay and Franz Josef Street and mingled with it. I began to bolt for home, but the procession was on us. The police car came first, then the car containing the Archduke Francis Ferdinand and his wife. I remember Count Harrach standing on the running board on the left-hand side of the car, shielding the Archduke with his body. It did not occur to me that such was his motive. It just seemed a gallant and genuinely Ruritanian way to ride.

The cars turned into Franz Josef Street. My kindly little friend leaned forward and fired twice. I was some distance from him and did not at first realize what he was doing. In 1914 we had not yet been educated by war and movies. Nothing spectacular happened, except that the Archduke leaned back and Sophie put her head on his knees. Then the wave of the crowd curved over Gabriel Princip. Above the bent heads and shoulders I could see Count Harrach put a handkerchief to the Archduke's mouth. It turned suddenly red as in a conjuring trick.

When I reached our door, the von Lechs and my parents came pouring out of it; they did not notice that I had joined them from the quay, not from inside the house. I never told them. I never told a word of my adventure at school. Guilt was already present, though it was many years before I admitted to myself that Gabriel Princip, seizing his opportunity, had used me to bluff his way through police and crowd to Franz Josef Street. Without me, he would have had to fire from some point on the Appel Quay past or through the protecting body of Count Harrach — a shot so long and hopeless that he would have drawn from his pocket only, perhaps, a cigarette.

The Idealist

HE STILL used to finger his captain's uniform and wonder
how the devil he had got into it without a major interrup-
tion of his life. There had been, of course, a sudden rush of
unfamiliar incidents, but no break in the continuity of the
self and the work which he knew, no chrysalis period of military training. At one moment he had been manager of a fleet
of barges on the gentle Severn; at the next he was an army
captain running lighters in a Mediterranean aflame with
war. A Deputy Assistant Director of Transportation they
called him. It seemed a long title. He was used to being
called the Young Boss. His father was the Old Boss.

And here he was in Piraeus harbor, emptying into his
barges the holds of the freighters which raced up from Alexandria; unloading on the quay or — if the weather were
kind — at little ports on the other side of the Corinth Canal;
storing and stacking; managing his Greek lightermen with
the aid of a foreman who, sober, much resembled his old
Severn-side foreman drunk; and commanding his small detachment of military through a sergeant-major who was the
recoil mechanism between himself and the Army. The sergeant-major took and distributed the shocks so that the
Young Boss — no, Captain Coulter, of course — could go

on doing his job without disrupting the still unintelligible organization of which he was a part.

Sergeant-Major Wrist was, in the eyes of Coulter, a character straight out of Kipling — pliant, resourceful, with as neat and tough a body as if he had polished and brushed it along with his equipment for twenty-five years of morning parades. He had managed to stay alive through one war already — not to speak of several expeditions which he described as picnics — and he freely expressed his intention of staying alive through this one. Coulter liked that. It was a proper old-soldierly way to talk. He felt that Wrist was wasted on a noncombatant job in the docks, and was sure that he must have pulled every possible regimental string to avoid it.

Their life of mere hard work was not, however, likely to continue undisturbed. That morning, April 6, 1941, Hitler had declared war on Greece. It was the end of five uncannily peaceful months while the Greeks fought only Italians, and the base had been free to pour in the sea-borne supplies from Egypt. Coulter did not think the Germans were likely to bomb Athens. Their pedantic minds would conceive that, at least, as sheer barbarism. But they were bound to have a shot, instantly, at knocking out the Piraeus.

He was still in his dockside office when the stroke came, alone with the sergeant-major who never objected — especially when they had first had an informal meal together and some drinks — to staying at leisurely work up to any hour of night. There was very little warning. When the sirens screamed, Sergeant-Major Wrist at once enjoined his captain to take refuge in the concrete shelter beneath the quay. Those, he said, were the Orders. A minute later, when they were at the door of the shelter, the raid began.

Coulter let the sergeant-major pop into the burrow, and himself stayed aboveground and watched. This, then, was war. Flame. Noise. Space geometry of searchlights and tracer. The upward flowering of explosions. The hammering and tinkling and whining of bits of metal. A mind quite arbitrarily prepared to lay long odds that its body stood in empty air between flying objects.

He was fascinated both by the scene and by the fact that his curiosity seemed to be greater than his fear. He had been just too young for the first war, and all his life had been envious of that experience which had destroyed a fifth of his near contemporaries at school. At the age of seventeen he had been conditioned to the prospect of death. Three weeks was the average fighting life of a British infantry subaltern on the western front, and he had been disappointed that he was just too young to take the gamble.

He knew all right that he had been a young fool — it had seemed to him in peace utterly incredible, this desire to immolate oneself for the sake of excitement — and yet, when a second war came along, it appeared that he was merely an older fool. He could perfectly well have been running barges in the unraided Severn instead of a port which — if there were anything in all the military theories he had read — was doomed to absolute destruction.

So this was all. Well, but to endure it for three weeks needed, no doubt, such sustained courage that one might welcome the end foretold by the military actuaries. All the same, it was exhilarating to find — after twenty years of wondering about it — that one wasn't particularly afraid. Coulter was annoyed at himself for this sudden vanity. What were a few bombs compared to forcing oneself to jump out of a trench into the steady, calculated fire of 1917? No. No, this wasn't the real thing.

It was over in ten minutes. A lucky string of bombs had erased the northern block of sheds and set the S.S. *City of Syracuse* on fire. Her crew — those few of them who were on board — had tumbled down the ship's brow and bolted for the dock gates as soon as she was hit. It wasn't surprising. In her holds were two hundred tons of explosives and ammunition. The ship's officers of course would know it, though it was possible that the crew, up to the moment they were ordered to clear out, did not. For the sake of security and to avoid the risk of devastating sabotage in a port where there had been German agents at large till the previous night, her cargo was officially described as mere military stores.

The *City of Syracuse* did not directly concern Coulter's office since she was discharging into the railway trucks alongside, not into lighters; but he had heard of the nature of her cargo and assumed that all the British working in the port were equally well informed. Security seemed to him to limit discussion rather than knowledge.

A naval launch was desperately trying to shift the ship into the outer harbor, but neither man nor rope could exist on her flaming bows, and the launch had not the power to tow her stern foremost. When the stern cable charred and broke, the Navy gave up. Very reasonably, too, thought Coulter.

The sergeant-major took his time in the shelter — and why not, since the all-clear had never sounded? — and missed such excitement as there had been. He now appeared, unruffled, at Coulter's elbow.

"Gone to fetch a tug, I expect, sir," he said, watching the launch scatter red foam from her bows as she slid away from the *City of Syracuse* into outer darkness.

"Perhaps," answered Coulter, giving the Navy the benefit of the doubt. "But the nearest tug is in the naval basin. It'll take her quarter of an hour to get here, and I think that's just ten minutes too long."

"She does seem to be burning pretty fierce, sir," Wrist agreed coolly.

Except for the occasional fountains of flame from the *City of Syracuse*, the docks were at peace under the moon. The tough central core of the northern sheds stood up sheer from a pile of rubble on which the dust was already settling. There were no troops about, for at that hour of night all of them, except the AA gunners, were back at their billets in the town. The duty clerks in the port offices were being marched away. The ambulances had cleared up the few wounded who could readily be found, and gone. The Greek fire brigades were presumably fully occupied in the town, for a glow over distant streets showed where another string of bombs had fallen.

As Coulter and Wrist turned to go, a staff car raced up the quay and stopped opposite to them. In it were the area commander and his adjutant, perfectly cool, perfectly dressed. God knew what they hoped to do there! If it came to that, thought Coulter, God knew why he was still there himself! Theirs presumably was a moral duty, but he hadn't any duty whatever. Some of his barges were adrift in the harbor, but he could only let them stay there until the Navy brought a tug.

"Good evening, Coulter," said the area commander. "Barging in again, I see."

It was a steady joke which pleased the commander very much. Somehow it pleased Coulter, too. It meant, after all, that the commander recognized him, liked him, knew what he did and appreciated it. And that could stand repetition.

"Anything we can do, sir?" he asked.

"If I were you," said the area commander, "I should get out of here pretty damn quick. There's nothing any of us can do."

He left his car and passed a pleasant word with the sergeant-major, even exchanging a casual reminiscence as one old soldier to another. Then he walked off on a tour of the docks to assure himself that there was no man in need of help.

"Well, he isn't taking his own advice, Sergeant-major, but we will," said Coulter, as if it were a foregone conclusion.

He started towards his waiting truck. Wrist pointed to the sliced cube of the northern building, outlined against the burning *City of Syracuse*.

"There was a gun up there, sir," he remarked. "I suppose they're all right."

It seemed to Coulter exceedingly unlikely that the gun crew would have cleared out leaving any of their number alive on top of the building. Still, it was just possible that the whole lot had been hit and forgotten, and that there might be a survivor in no state to climb down.

"Shall we go and see, sir?"

What particularly annoyed Coulter was that he knew just where and when his sergeant-major was likely to be a bit of a fraud. Indeed he doubted if you could become a sergeant-major at all without a keen appreciation of the value of eye-wash. He did not believe for a moment that Wrist would have made this intolerable and officious suggestion if it hadn't been for the presence, somewhere in the docks, of the area commander.

But there it was. That was the way an army fought. That was the value of leadership. Even if Wrist did take good care that there was someone to commend his act of gal-lantry, it only reflected tremendous credit on the area com-mander, who had inspired him. Scamps, these old soldiers? Well, if you liked. But, by God, they made the rules of their own game and enough of them had died at it!

The sergeant-major gave an indescribable hitch to his whole person, as if he were about to report to the Almighty that all, including his own well-polished soul, was present and correct. He then stepped out smartly towards the northern sheds. No, thought Coulter, of course he wouldn't run. Running, even forwards, suggested a sense of urgency and panic. That was not the way of the majestically profes-sional British Army.

Captain Coulter found himself unconsciously lagging half a step behind. That wouldn't do at all, and he drew up and paced stride for stride with Wrist. He cursed his lack of

any military training, aware as never before that he had
only been carried along by observing traditions of which
he had heard and read, by listening to the sergeant-major, by
a romantic enthusiasm for those unrealized three weeks of
youth.

What on earth was an officer expected to do in a case
like this? Use his common sense, he supposed. The situation
was not, in essence, very different from a pay parade when
you followed all the absurd little ceremonies because it was
expected of you, because it was that way a soldier liked to
work. Alternatively, it was doubtless in his power to order
the sergeant-major to drop this folly. Or he could go to
ground in any solid cover there might be, and charitably
watch Wrist trying to win his D.C.M. There was nobody
looking to see what he did himself.

"Oh, blast!" Coulter thought. "*I* am looking."

He found that he had grumbled the words half aloud,
and was startled by his own voice as much as by his superb
and unexpected arrogance.

"Sir?" asked the sergeant-major.

"Nothing. What the hell of a lot of bricks there are in four
walls!"

They clambered over the rubble of the shed, keeping the
mound so far as possible between themselves and the waves
of heat from the *City of Syracuse*. To Coulter's right was
the line of railway trucks waiting for the cargo they
were about — and instantaneously — to receive. For what
we are about to receive may the Lord make us truly thankful.
Some of them had been loaded that afternoon. No stenciling
on the boxes to indicate the contents. Security. Damned sol-

diers had learned that much if nothing else. At the tail end of the train, where there was neither building nor rubble between sidings and ship, the wood of the trucks was smoldering.

The flames over the *City of Syracuse* had died down. The plates of her upper works were red and the paint was curling off like wood shavings. All of her above the main deck was spurting and glowing. A subsidence or a melting anywhere would drop the furnace into the holds.

The cube of shed left upright was about thirty feet high. It stood because it had been reinforced to take the weight of the concrete gun platform on the roof.

"This will get us up, Sergeant-major."

A long strip of iron railing had been hurled against the trucks. It did not look as if it had fallen from anywhere, but as if it had been preserved on the ground for some calculable event of peacetime — to rail off the crowds at an embarkation of the royal family, or to fence a bit of welcoming garden in front of the customhouse. They up-ended the railing with some difficulty and leaned it against the wall for a ladder.

The heat of the burning ship seared eyes and face as Coulter looked over the top. On the platform was the gun, pointing at the scorched foremast of the *City of Syracuse* and partly wrenched from its mountings. There were two greatcoats, forming a vaguely human-shaped pile which aroused and disappointed the gallant zeal of the sergeant-major. There were the long, slender Bofors shells ready, arranged to be seized by their partners in the complicated dance of loading. The place was deserted. Well, what else could you expect? The officer in charge would have ensured — and of that Coulter had all along been certain — that none of his men was left up there alive.

"Time we were going, Sergeant-major," he said irritably.

"We'll just have a look-round in the rubble, sir."

"All right. It's possible, of course."

And he dutifully searched the hollows and dark corners where one of the gunners might have been blown. By this time he had become such a fatalist that he was jesting with the sergeant-major. To himself he said: Chum, you won't know a damn thing about it if the ship goes up, so why worry?

He clung to that unreasonably comforting thought until such time as Sergeant-major Wrist decided that honor was at last satisfied.

Coulter offered him a cigarette and walked back to his truck, which was parked outside the port offices. He could have run now with a clear conscience, but it did not seem worthwhile. He was neither courageous nor cowardly; he was just empty.

As they drove out of the dock gates, he said to the sergeant-major:

"Well, Mr. Wrist, if there are many chaps like you among the old regulars, I suppose we might win the war after all."

"Thank you, sir," replied the sergeant-major complacently. "There's one thing we're taught early, if I may say so, sir, and that's our duty to look after the men, sir."

They had gone half a mile from the docks when the *City of Syracuse* blew up. The blast cut a swathe through the houses packed on the hill above the port, but on the open sea front, along which they were driving, buildings merely spilled all their windows on to the pavement as neatly as if a stage set had fallen flat. Then a vast bulk, blacker than the night, swooped out of the sky before them and hurled up a waterlike spout of trees, earth and grass as it plunged into a little public park at the crossroads.

"Gawd, what was that?" the sergeant-major yelled.

"Must be the whole forepart of the *City of Syracuse*," Coulter answered, fascinated by such a colossal show of violence.

The bows and forecastle had pitched right way up, and immediately looked as if they had been on the site for years — a fitting decoration for the park of a seafaring people.

"Gawd!" exclaimed the horrified sergeant-major again. "She must have been full of ammo, and me muckin' about alongside like a bleedin' good Samaritan!"

"But I thought you . . ." Coulter began, and stopped.

Well, what was the use of saying that he thought Wrist knew, that he never dreamed he didn't know? However he put it, it would inevitably look like boasting. And he was sure — indeed he well remembered — that any unnecessary dwelling upon danger had not been considered a soldierly virtue by that lost generation whom he could never hope to equal.

Six Legs Are Welcome

IT's no good waving at them. Take this one, for example!
She'll get bored with crawling up my arm in a moment, and
fly off. For twenty-seven days in the month there's just the
usual mixture of insects, and on a twenty-eighth, for no reason at all, one species gets completely out of hand and fills up
all the available air.

No, I don't know what these are called — apart from their
Indian name. Odd-looking creatures, aren't they? Six legs.
Red and black asdic. And about an inch and a half of tor-
pedo tube in the stern. That's only a flying ant in your
gin. Just pick it out! There you are — neither of you one
penny the worse!

We'll go inside in another half hour when the mosquitoes
come on duty. But you needn't pay any attention at all to
these fellows. They're just satisfying their curiosity, with
only one day to do it in, perhaps.

Well, yes, there are limits. I quite agree. I don't hold with
those Buddhist chaps who won't squash a cockroach in case
it turns out to be their defunct mother-in-law. I've no fellow
feeling for any of the little pests. But if it hadn't been for
them I should be halfway through a life sentence now instead
of farming this wonderful place. A man can never quite forget a bit of luck like that. It's bound to influence him. Let

me get you another glass! That one's drowned herself. Weak heart, probably.

Live and let live — that's all I say. This bit of Paraguay belongs to them quite as much as to me. I'd better tell you the story. I haven't listened to myself speaking my own language for more than a year. And it will stop you imagining that something is crawling down the back of your neck when all you need, like the rest of us, is a haircut.

I was a mechanic in Argentina then, repairing tractors and managing the power plant and refrigeration on a big *estancia* up in the northeast corner of Corrientes. That's a strip of real white man's country — in between the marshes of the Paraná and the forests of Misiones. I liked the life and the people. Took to it from the start, like so many other Englishmen.

The nearest town was Posadas, where the train ferry crosses the Paraná from Paraguay to Argentina. I used to go there three or four times a year to keep an eye on the discharge of any of our machinery from the river steamers and arrange for its transport upcountry. You could drive a truck from Posadas to the *estancia* — just — but it was more comfortable to ride.

Posadas was not much of a town. A lot of dim lights, but no bright ones except the railway coaches and the Estrella de la Banda. The Estrella was a far better joint than you would have expected to find in a little river port, not at all the usual *pulpería* with a couple of half-witted girls in a dusty corner and drunks sleeping it off outside the door. Posadas had a small floating population of travelers between Paraguay and Argentina — some of them men of distinction or money, or even both — and Don Luis, who owned the Estrella, found it worth his while to feed them decently and provide entertainment. There were plenty of first-class passengers who made a point of staying the night, whenever they had to cross the Paraná, just in order to visit Don Luis's joint.

He was a big buck of an Italian — padded shoulders, local politics and all — but he was born in the *pampa* and he flattered himself that he was an Argentine of the Argentines. Anyone who addressed him as Luigi instead of Luis was safer the other side of the river. I knew him well enough to dislike him thoroughly. He didn't suspect it. You can go on detesting a man for years in Spanish so long as you have good manners. That's quite impossible in English.

There was a north wind blowing on that last visit of mine to Posadas. Just like today. It always brings the damp heat and the insects. And thirst. The boat from Buenos Aires had not arrived; so, instead of the drinks with the captain which I had been looking forward to, I went into the Estrella de la Banda. You could trust Luis's whisky. I'll say that for him.

It was early, and the place had not got going. Luis had a new girl.

"That's a little beauty!" I said to him.

She was not my sort, he told me. She was meant for traveling senators and so forth.

"She's only a mestiza," I said. "What's so special about her?"

He whispered to me what was special about her. I didn't believe him. But one of those senators off the international train might possibly want to believe him.

I sat down beside her. She wasn't more than seventeen,

and she was wearing a frock of innocent respectability just
like any young girl at her first party — except that it was
black. She had the wide, gentle face of the Indian, with
eyes far apart and hair growing low on the forehead; but
her mouth and her nose and all the rest of her were Spanish
of the loveliest. I couldn't get much out of her but *Sí, señor*
and *No, señor.* Very haughty indeed. Full of conventional
little parlor tricks. She wouldn't touch anything but lemonade. The line would have gone over very well in Buenos
Aires, but I thought she was overdoing it for Posadas, where
we all liked a bit of slap-and-tickle with, say, the third round
of drinks.

I spent an hour with her and then cleared out. I told Don
Luis he was right — that she wasn't at all the sort for a hard-
working man.

All the same I could not get her out of my mind. Her face
was so selfless and serious, too comfortable for a place like
the Estrella de la Banda. Not that there aren't some perfect
beauties about in cabarets, as well as in shops and offices.
But her type was different. I've often thought about it since,
and I can't put it better than this. You did not feel she was
bothering about being loved. She wanted to love. Her name
was Rosalinda Torres. But I couldn't guess much from that.
Rosalinda sounded professional. On the other hand, they
do like, out here in the backwoods, to give their daughters
high-sounding names.

There was no steamer next day, so I had nothing to do
but hang around in the heat and slap at all the life coming
down on the north wind, just like you chaps who travel
for pleasure. By the evening my curiosity was greater than

ever. I call it curiosity. But I thought I would be quite ready to take it to another table if young Rosalinda showed no interest in it.

She was sitting with the captain of the port, whom I did not like to interrupt for the sake of favors to come. However, he wasn't a wealthy man — in spite of all the help we shippers used to give him for the sake of his dear wife and children — and he soon got the same impression as I had the previous night. Meanwhile I was surprised to find myself a bit short with the other girls who wanted to share my whisky.

I had the sense to play up to Rosalinda's act. So, instead of beckoning or sending the waiter for her, I went over, hat in hand. She gave me a reasonably courteous little nod and indicated that I might sit down. We got on a little better until I told her that I was English. That closed her up tight. I gathered that foreigners were right out of her experience — as terrifying as a jaguar until you are sure it isn't hungry.

But I kept on treating her as if she had just been let out of the convent school for a day with uncle. I must have convinced her in the end that I, at any rate, wasn't hungry. Suddenly she burst out:

"I do not understand this place!"

"What's wrong with it?" I asked. "It's as good a place as there is till you get down to the Plata."

"It's not this way that a girl gets married," she answered.

One doesn't like to be fooled. I've knocked around the cabarets of two continents, and I expect you have, too. You never know what tricks those girls will be up to. I told myself firmly that I was not rich enough to be a senator and was too old to be sentimental.

"When did *you* leave the convent?" I asked, not making the irony too obvious.

"In May," she said.

It was a plain fact that she was stating.

"And your parents?"

Then it all came out — so far as she herself was capable of understanding what had happened to her. She had never come to grips with everyday life at all, you see. The forest, her parents, her simple education — those were all her past.

She was Paraguayan. Her parents, both of them, were of mixed Spanish and Indian blood. Humble folk, but true Americans and proud of it. They had managed to make a good living — and a little cash over — out of a remote holding up the river. No near neighbors but the forest Indians. As a matter of fact, their original farm was a part of this one. And it was a lot harder for them to reach by paddling than for you in your motor launch.

When Rosalinda came home from the convent at Asunción, she found that the land was going back to scrub, that the few peons had left, and that both her parents had been dead for over a month. Her brother, Hilario, was away in the Chaco, where the post was not nearly so reliable as word of mouth passed from settlement to settlement.

So there she was. Relations, none. Money, none. Food, what there was on the place. And then some fool, wanting to get her a free passage — but as likely as not he had no money either — put her on Don Luis's launch as a first step towards returning her to civilization. Luis was on his way down the Paraná from Brazil, and he had some woman with him — I never found out who it was — that he passed off as his wife.

Both of them, Rosalinda insisted, were angels to her. And when Luis suggested that, if she stopped off at Posadas, he would find her a husband, she believed him.

Can you imagine such simplicity? He would find her a husband, just like that. Well, after the war I gave up the sea — and me with my chief's ticket and a good job — because a Brazilian told me that he only needed a young partner, with lots of energy and a knowledge of machinery, to develop his diamond mine. What's the difference?

Don Luis cannot have expected that she would tell me so much. Or perhaps he didn't mind. Argentines never quite understand the Paraguayans, who are nearly all of mixed blood whatever class they belong to. He may have been looking at the girl the wrong way up.

Put it this way! He had picked up a destitute Indian girl with a little white blood; if he placed her well, it would be considered — by his friends and customers — a lot kinder than letting her starve in the forest.

But call her an ordinary Paraguayan girl, decently educated by poor parents who chose to live at the back of beyond, and the thing was an outrage on humanity!

I did not know what to say to her. I could not tell her on so short an acquaintance to jump on a horse and come to me if the going got really rough. She was far too lost to understand whom she could trust. And, anyway, it was a delicate subject to approach. I felt she was so blooming innocent that she might not know what she was in for. Of course she knew. Any woman would. But it had taken her a long time to put her uneasiness into definite thoughts which she could talk over with herself.

What I was really afraid of was her submissiveness. She was so used to doing what her parents told her and then what the nuns told her that she went and did what Don Luis told her. She had not grown up at all. If she stayed at the Estrella de la Banda for long, Indian resignation was going to overcome Spanish pride. That, no doubt, was what Luis reckoned.

"Do you want to go back to the convent?" I asked her.

"Not much," she said, giving me her first smile.

"What can you do to earn a living?"

"Cook," she answered, "and sew and look after a house."

Well, that was that! Like so many old-fashioned girls, she could spend the rest of her life as somebody's servant if she hadn't any money, or as somebody's wife if she had.

"Where are you living?"

"In a little house which Don Luis has lent me. There is a woman to look after me."

A real professional he was! The only mistake he made was to exhibit her in the Estrella. If he hadn't, she would never have seen that there was anything wrong at all. I doubted if I could even get any help from the parish priest. He wasn't a man of the world, and would hesitate to believe the libelous accusations of a red-hot heretic when Don Luis subscribed heavily to the Church and had provided the little waif with chaperon and all. As for the police, they would take the same point of view for less charitable reasons.

I had no intelligent suggestion to make — except that she should stick to lemonade — so I just sat with her till the place closed down, limiting my whisky to one every half hour and playing baby games with pencil and paper. Don Luis did not object. From time to time he would give me a grin and shake his head at me across the room. There was none of his high-class custom about.

The next afternoon the steamer arrived. By the time I had collected the electric pump I was waiting for and stowed it safely on a truck and had a meal, it was late and the Estrella was full. Besides the regulars there were a young Argentine off the train — very much the moneyed *señorito* — and a mixed bunch of passengers from the boat.

Don Luis had already fixed up Rosalinda with the likely young Argentine. She didn't know the conventions of the place, and she left her escort with a polite little bow and came straight over to my table. He stared murder, half rose and thought better of it. I was a much bigger man, wearing my working clothes with the flies buzzing round the sweat stains. He couldn't quite guess what he was up against. Mark you, I've said the Estrella was a high-class joint, and so it was, compared to the other places of so-called amusement along the Paraná; but to well-dressed young gentlemen fresh from Buenos Aires, we probably looked like a lot of customers who would stand no nonsense.

I was getting along splendidly with Rosalinda. Bless her heart, she had forgotten her troubles enough to be flirtatious! Just a matter of eyes, of course. Nothing that she wouldn't have done in her own home with proud mother looking on benevolently. And then she suddenly jumped up and cried:

"Hilario!"

We were sitting at a little table at the unfashionable end of the Estrella, near the angle of the bar and wall. Hilario's eyes must have been burning into us while he first watched from the entrance, and then walked the length of the room. It was the end of a long, desperate journey to his sister, during every hour of which he had imagined himself arriving too late. He did not kiss her or throw his arms round her. He was the kind of stern brother you read about in the Old Testament. I was his first objective. He said to me:

"Outside!"

Rosalinda evidently thought this was the proper way for a brother to behave. She made no attempt to touch him until she had loosed off some quick explanations in Guarani. They had been brought up together in the loneliness of the forest, those two, and words were hardly necessary to them at all. A half sentence, an exclamation, a tone of voice could tell far more essentials than the usual forms of speech which you and I go through. Hilario begged me to forgive him, and, if I could not see my way to forget an unjust insult, to wait for him a little while until he had obliged the gentleman responsible for his agitation.

He was only about eighteen and looked extraordinarily like his sister — the same gentle, tender face with the features a little sharper and the mouth a little thinner. He was wearing the old-fashioned hat and poncho which you might see in Posadas on a *fiesta*. On working days, however, we wore coats and trousers like anyone else, with a few individualities in the way of boots and belts. Hilario and his manners belonged to the Latin America of the last century.

"Which is this Don Luis of whom I have heard?" he asked me.

He felt it indelicate even to mention the name to his sister. Luis had just come in from the kitchen — about the only place where his personal influence never did anything but good — and was standing near the other end of the bar, staring at the new arrival. He must have guessed who Hilario was — the resemblance to Rosalinda was so marked — but probably reckoned that a half-Indian boy, with a face made for women and the guitar, was not likely to give him much trouble.

They met in the upper half of the dance floor, and Hilario called him exactly what he was. Luis's knife was out before the second syllable. I don't know whether you have ever seen our upcountry fighting. *Srrr! Click! Ssssh!* And it's all over. One moment Luis was as fast as a hornet's sting, and the next moment he was lying on the floor with his works coiling out around him and the flies beginning to come in from the kitchen. He had courage. He did not complain. That sort of thing was an occupational risk, I suppose.

Hilario's face was still soft and courteous. He might have been apologizing to the company for some outrageous favor which he had felt bound to extend to Don Luis. He had cut upwards and his hand had followed the knife. The blood was running down from his fist to the blade and dripping on the floor. You could hear it. That flash of red and silver under the hard white light hypnotized everyone into silence for a second or two. Rosalinda was already behind her brother — though I don't quite know how she had got there. It was the only safe place in the whole world for her. She knew that instinctively.

No one — except Rosalinda — had moved yet, but Hilario had not a hope of reaching the front door. He backed towards the kitchen entrance alongside the bar. Out to his right flank the barman reached for a gun. We didn't normally use such things in Posadas. It was the bar revolver — kept under the counter for emergencies alongside the lemons and the dishwater. I don't believe in getting mixed up in foreign rows like a drunken fireman. Still, what was I to do? Hilario was the only chap who could produce a satisfactory solution for Rosalinda.

The barman was half turned away from me, and the soda-water siphon took him over the right ear. It was far too forcible a way of expressing my sympathies with a murderer's sister, but I had nothing else handy. Disastrous! I tell you, I knew while that siphon was still in the air that the only future for me in Argentina was a long jail sentence.

That broke the spell. A woman screeched. The room rose at us. The customers might have shrugged their shoulders and attended to their business, such as it was, if this affair had merely been a difference of opinion between two of them about an Estrella girl. But Don Luis was a prominent citizen, and he had been so very thoroughly killed.

If I'd had half a chance I would have slipped through the kitchen door and bolted. But Hilario and Rosalinda were blocking it. I caught a glimpse of the cook — he was a Syrian and a sensible man — sailing out through the window, and then I found myself cast for the part of Horatius on the Bridge while Hilario shoved Rosalinda out at the back and told her to run.

I wasn't alone long enough for any heroism. I remember smashing a bottle on somebody, and getting in a right hook which hurt me quite as much as the other fellow. Then a chair broke on my head. I suppose the leg was rotten. Fortunately for me, Don Luis had never succeeded in keeping termites out of the furniture. I went down and, for an instant, out. The next thing I knew was Hilario dragging me out of the kitchen into the open.

That appalling knife of his seemed a bit wetter round the point, and he had managed to slam and lock the door behind us. The pursuit — this was all a matter of seconds — had not yet had time to disengage and run round the block to the back of the Estrella. There were only some shanties and a lane between us and the riverbank; as soon as we were clear of them and had collected Rosalinda I was running rather than staggering.

After paddling himself across the Paraná, Hilario had left his canoe about two miles downstream. He hadn't stopped to think. Indeed he had not thought at all during his journey on foot and horse and rail and river right across the length of Paraguay; he was just a moving blaze of anger. Posadas police hardly entered into his calculations at all. They preferred to spend their nights in decent gentlemanly idleness — but once their attention had been drawn to any undesirable character trying to escape from Argentina to Paraguay, stopping him was a routine job. They knew the riverbank so thoroughly that they could count on picking us up and returning to their bottles before wives or waiters had time to clear away.

The night was dark, but one can see by starlight in these parts and spot a moving figure at twenty-five yards so long as it does move. There was no cover at all along the flood plain of the Paraná. Worse still, there were creeks and patches of marsh so that we could never race off into the

Americas at large or even get very far from the tracks. To my mind our chance of reaching Hilario's canoe was nil.

We just bolted along the riverbank until we were stopped by a creek. We had to follow it up to its head, and that lost us our lead. Once round the creek, we had a choice of three tracks westwards — one north of a marsh and one south, and a third which ran down to the sands. We heard horses already cantering out from Posadas, and there was no time at all for hesitation.

We took the middle track north of the marsh. The going was good, and Rosalinda didn't hold us back. She was not even shocked by all this savagery. Murder didn't count when it was right. Just another example of her extraordinary innocence. She had kicked off her shoes and was running as free as a little twelve-year-old. Her education had not lasted long enough to soften the soles of her feet.

But it was the shoes which gave us away. The police troopers spotted them, lying bang in the middle of the right track. They did not have to split up and do a bit of scouting. They came on behind us like a charge of cavalry.

There was a small patch of open plain by the side of the track, and we dropped flat on it. When the pursuit — six of them — had thundered past, I began to have hopes of getting clear. The obvious move was to return to the head of the creek and try one of the other two routes. We had just reached the junction when back came the police. They must have reached some point — a customs post, I think — beyond which we could not have passed. Three of them were riding south of the marsh, and three north — at the same time quartering the narrow strip of plain where we had lain down and covering the third track to the sands.

In the direction of Posadas were more lights, carried by such of the sporting citizenry as were attracted by the chance of a free shot at human game. No hope for us there, either — so we cut down into the angle between the creek and the Paraná where our first dash from the town had landed us.

The whole of the hunt gradually converged upon our corner. I thought this was an unfortunate accident until a launch drifted down from Posadas and began to search the water's edge with its light to prevent us from swimming away. The police knew exactly where we were. Long experience and elimination of all the possibilities.

"Why do they not bring nets?" Hilario whispered bitterly. He was hurt at being treated as something only fit for the taxidermist. After all, he knew that he was a harmless and honorable boy on all occasions when convention did not call for murder.

The advancing line, with one flank on the Paraná and the other on the creek, became shorter as it approached us. There was not a hope of breaking through. To judge by the lights, the gap between man and man was about forty yards and rapidly lessening. It was then that I began to see stars, and ascribed them to the crack I had received over the skull. It's not what a man really feels which finishes him, but what he thinks he feels. Just because there was a sickening, patternless mess of lights in front of my eyes, I was ready to pass out. I told Rosalinda and Hilario to slip through the line if they saw the remotest chance, and leave me.

They were whispering excitedly in Guarani, and seemed unreasonably hopeful.

"But why? Why give up now?" Rosalinda asked me.

There was a sob of disappointment in her voice, just as if I had refused her something which she had set her heart on, when all the rest of her world agreed.

I tried to pull myself together, and noticed that some of the lights, instead of dancing in front of my eyes, were stationary in Rosalinda's hair.

Then I understood. There had been a hatch of fireflies on the river flats. The muggy weather and the hot north wind had brought on the one day in twenty-eight that I was telling you about. They might have been ants or flies or these savage-looking fellows which you seem to have forgotten about for the moment; but they happened to be beetles — fireflies.

Beautiful? I don't know whether it was or not. It was mad. I tell you that there wasn't a cubic foot of air — literally — without a firefly in it. You couldn't see. No wonder I thought I was fainting! It was like — well, I've often tried to describe it to myself. Imagine yourself infinitely small and suspended in a cylinder of gas! Imagine the hot molecules rushing about and cannoning into each other. No, it wasn't beautiful.

The three troopers on the left of the line had been following the bank of the creek. They were now so close that we didn't dare whisper. Not that they would have heard us. They were cursing and damning and waving their hats about. Quite useless, but it's a human instinct to try to clear a space in front of the eyes. Their horses were nervous and giving any amount of trouble. I doubt if they were in the least bothered by the fireflies; they had caught the exasperation of their riders, as horses always do.

Hilario started to squirm forward foot by foot, and Rosalinda and I followed. You couldn't tell where the police troopers were going, fighting their horses in that damned silly way instead of showing confidence. One of the poor beasts was just about to tread on me when it saw me. It shied, and its rider's language was worse than ever. He did not look at the ground. He was trying to pierce the intolerable flickering on a level with his eyes.

It was perfectly safe to stand up and run as soon as we were past them. At the head of the creek we took the track down to the sands and reached Hilario's canoe by swimming and wading.

Of course I can never go back to Argentina, but who cares? Three thousand acres I farm here. When Hilario showed me this place and its own private river with a flow of three hundred thousand gallons a minute and an even drop of twenty feet in half a mile, I saw what could be done in the way of power plant and refrigeration. It wouldn't suit everyone. But we often have visitors like yourself. And they are very welcome whether they have two legs or six. Hilario himself always preferred mining to farming. He has done very well at it.

Rosalinda? Well, they get a bit full in the figure, you know. But does that matter when the only face you ever want to look at is on top of it? Our boys made her go out fishing this afternoon. They'll be back any moment. Certainly before the mosquitoes start. Well, yes, if you look at it that way, I suppose they have started. But don't go slapping at them! Round here nobody has ever died of fever since her poor mother and father.

Roll Out the Barrel

MARGIT was an island like the rest of us. In the set of complicated currents she kept her shores intact only by loyalty to what was best in herself. She had not much else to be loyal to.

She was a Hungarian peasant who had earned her lonely living as a servant in Budapest ever since she was fourteen years old. Social democracy and a husband with a bit of land — those were her desires, political and personal. Towards the present regime she was dully neutral, for it snatched away with one hand what it gave with the other.

She took pride in her skill, and as much in her employers as they permitted. For the last six months she had worked for a middle-aged consulting engineer, respectable and law-abiding. He seldom laughed, and his ready smile seemed to spring from a natural courtesy rather than any personal interest. He left no doubt, however, that he appreciated her cooking, and that was enough for Margit.

She used to daydream — failing a better subject — that he had asked her to be his wife, though any woman could see that he was dedicated to something, perhaps the memory of a former love, more distant than marriage. The dream never lasted longer than the washing-up of two plates and a coffee cup.

Margit knew very well that she hadn't the beauty to re-
vive a dead heart. All her mirror told her was that she was
squat and thick and brown; it could not reveal that her eyes
were gay and that she moved with light feet and a provoca-
tive swing of the skirt. That touch of gallantry had been
born of the czardas danced in the village of her girlhood,
and was kept alive by the barrel of excellent wine in the
kitchen.

The barrel was a present from her brother, who had inherited the little family vineyard and contrived to hold
back enough of the harvest to supply himself and her. The
rest went to the state cellars for export. Margit was puzzled
that wine should have become so scarce and expensive. In
the days before the war a generous employer would no
more have thought of reckoning up what was drunk in the
kitchen than of counting the potatoes.

So Margit treasured her hundred-liter barrel. She wasn't
a heavy drinker. At the moderate rate of a big glass for
lunch and another for supper, there was only enough to
keep her morale more gay than grim for about two hundred days. The barrel, too, was a symbol. It brought into
the worried city a sense of solidarity with her village — a
spiritual rather than political class-consciousness. She felt
for her hundred liters the welcome that a businesswoman
would give to a hamper of flowers from the garden of her
first lover.

Some of her treasure, of course, she had to share; but
that, too, was joy. She was enabled to be gracious and to
indulge the aristocrat that lived in her peasant heart. So,
when she received a visit from the well-dressed gentleman

who had recently begun to sit outside the café at the corner, it was hospitality rather than fear which made her draw a jug for him.

She knew what he was. Among the humble there was unspoken alliance for the recognition of secret police. The porter of the block, who that very day had been ordered by the well-dressed gentleman to give him a weekly bulletin of information, had dutifully kept the secret, but handed out broad hints to chosen friends.

The policeman in Margit's kitchen was a very superior specimen of the breed — not at all the type which normally collected information from porters. She greeted him with the politeness reserved for a class above her own, and hovered hospitably over him.

"Good wine, this!" exclaimed the gentleman from the café at the corner, stretching his legs under the table. "Is your employer rich?"

"My brother sent it me," she replied. "It has nothing to do with the master."

"And what does he drink himself over there?" — the visitor jerked a thumb towards the narrow passage which led, through a faintly delicious atmosphere of spices and onions, to the office and dining room of Margit's consulting engineer.

"Whatever he can get, sir."

"And plenty of it, eh?"

The visitor, determined to be a democrat, pinched her playfully. Margit's reception of the compliment was cold. She knew from experience that her rotundities were eminently pinchable, and she did not — for example, with the porter — take offense. But the caress of her visitor was incorrect; he made it appear a studied gesture rather than an irresistible temptation.

Margit dropped her best manner and answered him with a rough frankness. That was one good thing about the present regime. You needn't — if you belonged to the proletariat — bother with ceremony when you didn't feel inclined.

"How can anyone get plenty of it?"

"Complaining of the regime, are you?"

"Listen, I'm a peasant! Better off, worse off? I don't know. Wait and see — that's what we say."

"What about the visitors here? Is that what they say?"

"Do you think I've nothing to do, cocky, but crawl up the passage and listen at the door?"

The visitor gave a hoarse chuckle, into which Margit's wine and pleasant, broad accent had injected some sincerity. "We come from the same district," he exclaimed. "I see that!"

"Every district has some black pigs among the white."

"That's the end, sweetheart," he said — quite tolerantly, but as if the inevitable time had come to exchange good-fellowship for his normal business attitude. "Sit down!"

Resignedly she sat down opposite him at the kitchen table. He represented the limitless power of the state. There was no need for him to explain or threaten, and they both knew it.

He drew from his pocket three photographs of the same man: full face, right profile and left profile.

"Have you ever seen that one?" he asked her.

"No."

"Have you ever heard the name of Istvan Sarvary?"

"No. Who's he?"

"An enemy of our country, my girl. A revolutionary and warmonger. And at last I'm on his track. Look at those photos, and take your time."

Margit obeyed. The police photographs were clear, glossy prints, upon which every detail could be seen. The subject looked like an unwashed criminal, hollow-cheeked, sneering and obstinate. She did not recognize the face. Then, in the left profile, she noticed the man's glasses. They were round, old-fashioned and of heavy tortoise shell, and there was a homemade repair just in front of the left ear, where the rivet, or binding, had been wrapped in some soft substance to prevent rubbing.

A possible identity for Sarvary at once occurred to her. Yet it was so unlikely that there was no sudden start of recognition in her eyes or mouth for the trained interrogator across the table to leap upon.

"You are interested?" he suggested.

"You told me to take a long look."

"And what do you see?"

What she saw in the eye of the mind was a drawer in the consulting engineer's dressing table and a pair of old glasses with the left bar wrapped round by a neatly sewn strip of wash leather. Could they be the same glasses? Was it possible for a haggard, clean-shaven man with dark, wavy hair to turn into her employer with his well-rounded cheeks, his straight white hair greased firmly back, and his white luxuriant mustache which looked as if it had been over his mouth for the last thirty years?

Then there was his nose. The man in the photograph had a strong, fleshy nose, quite ordinary. Her employer had a Roman nose with a marked and distinguished bump on its bridge. The shape of it, she remembered — almost with a giggle — seemed to change in hot weather. No, of course it was unthinkable. Her kind master could not be a man wanted by the police, a barbarian trying to bring about another war.

"I've seen someone like him," she said at last.

She couldn't tell how much her face had given away. Something, yes. The keen peasant game of buying and selling was in her blood. She knew, from the parallel of the market place, that her hesitation had been too long and that she must explain it.

"Who?"

"The new notary of our village."

"They have a queer breed in your village," he remarked contemptuously. "Stop fooling, girl! When did this man come to see your employer?"

"Never."

"Then what was he doing — the person whom you thought the photograph resembled?"

"Our notary? He makes too much money at home to come to Budapest."

The visitor rose from the table and brutally dominated her eyes.

"If you hurt me, I'll scream," she threatened. "They know I'm respectable here."

"Hurt you? My dear, we don't do that sort of thing. I'm just going to give you time to remember."

The gentleman from the corner café strolled impassively across the kitchen and turned on the tap of the barrel. The thin, fast stream of wine hit the tiles with a neat splash.

Margit shrieked, and leaped for the tap rather than for him. At once she made brutal contact with her chair again, arms bruised, bewildered by the dexterity with which she had been flung back.

"We like wine in our district, don't we?" he said. "Barrel full?"

"Yes. Yes, sir," she begged. "Nearly full."

"Then it will take about ten minutes to empty it. Plenty of time to talk."

The purple and pink foam that had jumped from the tiles subsided, and the lake of wine deepened and spread.

"Please, sir! Please!"

"But I shall be delighted to turn it off when you've told the truth. A pity for such good wine to be wasted! I should say your brother's is a rather stony soil facing south," he replied, talking with an exasperating slowness.

"It didn't remind me of the notary. I swear it," she sobbed, the big tears ricocheting off her apron into wine.

"Ah? Of whom, then?"

"Nobody. I was impertinent. I've never seen the face before."

"And the name Istvan Sarvary? Have you never heard it?

Or overheard it, perhaps? Think now! That's a generous tap you have there."

"No, never! Never, sir! I've never heard it."

The words were loud and incoherent with grief. The lake of wine found out an imperceptible slope and began to run towards the passage. At the door it deepened to a quarter of an inch, and the color changed from a pink transparency to black with red reflections.

"He might have come here without you knowing it?"

"Yes, yes, of course he might," she answered eagerly.

"You're not sure that you haven't seen him, then?"

"No. How could I be sure?"

"Then we have only to take a little step further. Look! I'm just going to shut off the tap. Tell me when it was he might have come here — that's all I want to know."

Margit was utterly muddled. What he invited her to say sounded so reasonable. Why on earth was she letting her wine run away when she had only to tell him a date, a movement, her crazy suspicion, anything? Yet — she didn't tell lies.

She opened her mouth and nothing would come. All the inhibitions of the Christian Europe that had made her stood in the way. Had she been asked outright whether her employer could be Istvan Sarvary she might at least have answered that she had wondered. Might have. But there again, standing at the gate, was all the loyalty of a feudal system that had vanished and left nothing but its good behind.

"I can't tell you. I don't know."

The interrogator kept the barrel running.

"Won't, little one, not can't! Won't, you mean."

She heard the front door open and shut as her employer came home.

"Good heavens, what's all this?" he exclaimed.

He bounded up the passage on the track of the wine, and caught the visitor with his hand still on the tap.

"Margit, your wine! What's all this?"

Margit's face was bedabbled with tears. The gentleman looked confused and guilty.

"Tap leaking?" the consulting engineer asked.

"He turned it on," she sobbed.

"Friend of yours?"

"No, no, no!"

"Well, then — ah, I think I understand! But, my dear sir, if you had anything to ask, why didn't you come to see me? I know everyone in the building and my reputation is sound, I hope. No good telling you I'm a party member — too old, for one thing. But what I always say is, they're doing fine work for Hungary. Example to all Europe, eh? We're both patriots, aren't we? Well, there's the bond. Now you put me through the hoops in any way you like."

Her master was so friendly and natural that Margit at once put out of mind that imagined identity. After all, there was more than one pair of mended spectacles in the world. And then his nose! You couldn't alter a nose that God had made.

"What do *you* know of Istvan Sarvary?" the visitor shot straight at him.

"Sarvary? Why, I thought he was abroad. Don't tell me the swine has managed to get back to Budapest!"

"He was a friend of yours, was he?"

"No, he wasn't. Far from it! But you've come to the right shop, my dear sir. I'll answer all your questions. We can't have men like Istvan Sarvary about. Margit, there's nothing to drink in the house. May we borrow what's left in the barrel? I'll make it up to you. We'll try to get something as good as yours."

"You're generous," the gentleman sneered suspiciously.

"You think so? I'll tell you how it is. I don't want the state to show pity. Try the dogs, shoot them, exile them, put them to work! They're expendable, aren't they? But a little woman like this — well, when she gets in the way, the state can't help it and mustn't show pity. Never! But chaps like you and me are free to do what we can. That's what I say."

Margit didn't agree at all with this view of the state, but she assumed it was politics and over her head. If a man with a good heart accepted cruelty, it meant nothing and was just words.

The man from the corner café took Margit's employer a little aside and warned him of something in a low voice.

"She? Oh, I don't think she could have seen him. But you never know. Well, if there's anything at all, you'll get it out of her. Better methods than wine taps, eh?

"Now let's sit down. It must be seldom that you get a real hot tip straight from the horse's mouth and a jug of first-class stuff to go with it. If you don't mind my saying so, I've watched the scent of that wine making you more human every minute."

The visitor grinned, then pulled himself together with

military solemnity and declared that he had no time for gossip.

"This gossip is going to be worth your while, Captain. I'll tell you for a start one man whom Sarvary is likely to be seeing — his wife's cousin. You didn't know that, did you? And you're in charge of the investigation."

"Not yet," the visitor admitted, "but I shall be. It's every man for himself in the police, and I like to wait for the best minute to put in my report. Now you help me, and I won't forget you. What would you say if I told you I'm on to a connection between Sarvary and this very house?"

"Your very good health!" exclaimed the consulting engineer, raising his glass. "Is that so? Well, well, now let me see! First of all I'll fix up my Margit, and then I'm with you. I can't have such a cook upset," he explained. "You can't expect a little artist to work without a drink in her heart. Look here, sweetheart, here's an address! You go there and tell them to deliver another barrel of red this evening. And you must need a rest after all this. Take the afternoon off if you want to."

He scribbled a note and gave it to Margit. She had never seen her employer so cordial. She was hurt that he had never smiled at her as genuinely as he was smiling at this filthy crook from the corner café, and hurt, too, even if she were to be compensated, that the pair of them should calmly sit down and drink up the rest of her wine. She said to herself that it was unfeeling. Just unfeeling, that was all. Not even enough to excuse a toss of the head.

"But I can't stop long," the visitor protested. "I don't want to take my eyes off this street."

"Splendid! Splendid! It's good to know that our safety is in your hands. But why not telephone one of your sergeants and tell him to check all movements in and out of this house in your absence? A good chance to see whether he knows his job! He won't know you are here and you can watch him through the curtains."

Margit put her kerchief over her head and went out, leaving the two to their sly grins and good-fellowship. It was just like men, she thought, to sit down and souse on somebody else's wine and pretend they were catching enemies of the state. It didn't make any difference — townee or peasant, consulting engineer or Communist, they were all the same. Wine and pinching people where people were roundest and sacrificing the helpless.

She delivered her employer's note at the address he had given her. It was a cheerless, obscure, commercial office without the heartening smell of liquor or the noisy group of customers welcome to try out many more vintages than they ever meant to buy. Well, nothing was sold any longer as, traditionally, it ought to be sold.

She called on a friend who might have comforted her, but wasn't in. Boozing too, probably. Then she idled away the afternoon in public gardens and at a public meeting. After two hours she went home. It was all very well to tell her to take the afternoon off, but who would get the supper, she would like to know.

Her employer was asleep. The gentleman from the corner café had gone. Neither of them had made any attempt to mop up the lake of wine and its meandering streams, so she set to work on the kitchen. She forced herself (for she was economical) to dip a fine white cloth in the deepest pool and to squeeze it into a glass in case the wine should be still drinkable. It certainly wasn't. She was ashamed and determined to clean her floor much more thoroughly than usual, especially after chopping meat.

Then three hefty men brought up her new barrel. They did not talk much, and they would not accept a drink. They weren't at all like the deliverymen she used to know. The three rolled away the old barrel down the passage. She wondered what wood her brother was using for staves. But perhaps the barrel seemed so heavy because the deliverymen didn't get enough to eat. That must be it. In these days they made criminals into policemen and boys of good family into porters.

After that, all the tides of complication receded from her little personal island.

There was a flurry of nervousness when some police came to inquire about the gentleman from the corner café, who, it seemed, had disappeared. Her kind employer told her not to be frightened of them but to describe her interrogation just as it had happened.

"The only thing I shouldn't say if I were you, Margit," he warned her, "is that the man stayed on a little here after he telephoned his sergeant that he had gone. We don't want him to make trouble for us when he turns up again, do we?"

So Margit said nothing at all of that, and the police found the incident of the wine tap so comic that they paid very little attention to her. She disapproved of their behavior. It was typically masculine and insensitive. But — taking the rough with the smooth, as she put it — she couldn't complain. The new barrel of wine did not carry in it the love of a brother, but at least she would be able to taste, whenever she sat down to her meals, the remarkable generosity of her master.

The Greeks Had No Word for It

"May I say ten pounds?" the auctioneer asked. "Five? Thank you, madam. . . . Six. . . . Six, ten. . . . Seven. . . . Seven, ten. . . . At seven pounds, ten. Going at seven pounds, ten. An ancient Greek drinking bowl of the best period. Going at . . ."

Sergeant Torbin had at last wandered into the auction because there was nothing else to do. It was early closing day in Falkstead, and the shops were shut. There was nowhere to sit but the edge of the quay, and nothing to watch but the brown tide beginning to race down to the North Sea between gray mudbanks. The only sign of animation in the little town was around the open front door of a small boxlike eighteenth-century house, the contents of which were being sold.

"Eight!" said the sergeant nervously, and immediately realized that nothing could give a man such a sense of inferiority as a foreign auction.

But the atmosphere was quiet and decorous. The auctioneer acknowledged Bill Torbin's bid with a smile which managed to express both surprise and appreciation at seeing the United States Air Force uniform in so rural a setting.

He might have been welcoming him to the local church hall.

"May I say eight, ten?"

A military-looking man, overwhelming in size and manner, nodded sharply.

Bill could hardly hope that the bowl was genuine. He liked it for itself. Angular black figures chased one another round the red terra-cotta curve. He recognized Perseus, holding up that final and appalling weapon, the Gorgon's head. Very appropriate. A benevolent goddess, who reminded Bill of his tall, straight mother, looked on approvingly.

He ran the bowl up to ten pounds. When the auctioneer's hammer was already in the air, he heard someone say:

"Guinness!"

There was a snap of triumph in the word, a suggestion that the whole sale had now come to a full stop. It was the military man again. To Sergeant Torbin he was the most terrifying type of native — a bulky chunk of brown tweed suit, with a pattern of orange and gray as pronounced as the Union Jack, and a red face and ginger mustache on top of it.

"It's against you, sir," the auctioneer told him hopefully.

Bill knew that much already. But the mysterious word Guinness sounded as if it had raised the ante to the moon. He panicked. He decided that he had no business in auctions. After all, he had only been in England a week and had come to Falkstead on his first free afternoon because it looked such a quiet little heaven from the train.

"Going at ten guineas. . . . At ten guineas. . . . Sold at ten guineas!"

Hell, he ought to have guessed that! But who would think that guineas would pop up at auctions when they belonged in the time of George III? Bill Torbin walked out and sat on the low wall which separated the garden from the road, conducting a furious auction with himself while he waited for the six-thirty train back to his bleak East Anglian airfield.

He had just reached the magnificent and imaginary bid of one hundred goddam guineas when the tweed suit rolled down the garden path with the drinking bowl under its arm.

"Nice work, Colonel!" Bill said, for at last he had an excuse to talk to somebody.

"Oh, it's you, is it? I say, you didn't want it, did you?"

The sergeant thought that was the damn silliest question he had ever heard. He realized, however, that it was meant as a kind of apology.

"British Museum stiff with 'em!"

Again he got the sense. The Englishman was disclaiming any special value for his purchase. Bill asked if the bowl were genuine.

"Good Lord, yes! A fifth-century Athenian cylix! The old vicar had it vetted. His father picked it up in Istanbul during the Crimean War. That was the late vicar's late niece's stuff they were selling. Have a look for yourself!"

Sergeant Torbin took the bowl in his hands with reverent precautions. Round the bottom, which he had not seen before, two winged horses pulled a chariot. He wondered what on earth he would ever have dared to do with so exquisite a piece if he had bought it. He might have presented it to the squadron, but, like himself, the squadron had no safe place to keep it.

"How the devil did you know I was a colonel?"

Bill did not like to say that he couldn't possibly be anything else unless it were a general, but he was saved by the bell. The church clock struck six.

"Ah, they'll be opening now," said the colonel with satisfaction. "How about a drink?"

Bill Torbin murmured doubtfully that his train left at six-thirty. The colonel announced that Falkstead station was only two minutes from the pub, and that he himself had often done it in eighty seconds flat. Considering the noble expanse of checked waistcoat, Bill thought it unlikely. But you never knew with these tough old Englishmen. Half of the weight might be muscle.

The colonel led the way to The Greyhound. It was a handsome little pub, built of white weather-boarding with green shutters, but Torbin had no eyes for it. He was watching the precious cylix, which was being swung by one of its handles as carelessly as if it had been a cheap ash tray. The sergeant decided that the British had no reverence for any antiquities but their own.

In the bar were four cheerful citizens of Falkstead drinking whisky, two boatbuilders drinking beer with the foreman of the yard and, at a table near the window, the auctioneer and his clerk keeping up respectability with The Greyhound's best sherry. The colonel, disconcertingly changing his manner again, greeted the lot of them as if he had just arrived from crossing the North Sea singlehanded, and enthroned the cylix on the bar.

"What have you got there, Colonel Wagstaff?" the inn-keeper asked.

"That, Mr. Watson, is a Greek drinking bowl."

"Never saw 'em used," Mr. Watson answered, "not when I was a corporal out there."

Wagstaff explained that it was an old one, which possibly had not been used for two thousand years.

"Two thousand, four hundred," said the auctioneer, taking his pipe out of his mouth, "at the very least."

"Time it was!" Mr. Watson exclaimed heartily.

"What are you going to put in it?" the colonel asked.

"Who? Me?" Watson said, not expecting to be taken literally.

"But you can't start drinking out of it!" Bill protested.

"It's what it is for, isn't it?"

"And an unforgettable experience for our American friend," said the auctioneer patronizingly, "to drink from the same cup as Socrates — or at any rate someone who knew the old boy."

"Well, seeing as it's this once," Mr. Watson agreed, "what would you say, Colonel?"

"That Burgundy which you bought for the summer visitors is quite drinkable."

The cylix was about two inches deep, and just held the bottle which Mr. Watson emptied into it. The terra cotta flushed under the wine. The figures blossomed.

"See?" said Colonel Wagstaff. "Like rain in a dry garden!"

The company gathered round the bar. Wagstaff raised the bowl in both hands and took a hearty pull.

"Tastes a bit odd," he remarked, passing it on to Torbin. "Still, you can't have everything."

The loving cup went round the eleven of them and Mr. Watson.

"Fill her up again," said the auctioneer.

The next round was the colonel's, and after that there was a queue for the fascinating honor.

"If you take the seven-forty-five bus to Chesterford," Colonel Wagstaff suggested, "there's sure to be a train from there."

Bill was beginning to feel for the first time that England had human beings in it. But it was not the facile good-fellowship which persuaded him to wait for the bus. The bowl had become a local possession, and The Greyhound a club in which he was welcome to drink but might not pay. He was jealous. He could not bring himself to leave his goddess skittering along the bar in pools of Burgundy without his own hands ready to catch her.

The auctioneer said a fatherly good-by to all, trod upon his bowler hat and left. Bill was astonished at the dignity with which he ignored his oversight and knocked out the dent. He looked at the clock. He felt bound to mention that it was seven-forty.

"By Jove, so it is!" said the colonel, taking his mustache out of the bowl.

Till seven-forty-five he addressed them shortly on the value of punctuality in the military life, and then they all piled out into the street, led by Colonel Wagstaff, the bowl and Sergeant Torbin, and cantered through the village to the yard of the drill hall, where the Chesterford bus was waiting.

It was a typical, dead, East Anglian bus stop on the edge of the North Sea marshes. The bus was not lit up, and there was no sign of the driver. The colonel swore it was a disgrace and that Sergeant Torbin would never catch his train at Chesterford.

"What time does it go?" Bill asked.

"I don't know. But you might very easily miss it. It's a damned shame! Here's a gallant ally trusting conscientiously to the Chesterford Corporation to get him to camp before midnight, and he lands in the guardroom because their bloody buses can't run to time! I've a good mind to teach them a lesson. Anybody want to go to Chesterford?"

About half a dozen of them agreed that it would be a reasonable act of protest to run the bus themselves, whether they wanted to go to Chesterford or not.

Wagstaff opened the driver's door and switched on all the lights. Bill was fresh from a lecture in which he had been told to behave in England with the formality of the English. He decided that he had better be American and hire a car. But the colonel had tossed the bowl onto the driving seat and was just about to sit on it. Bill rescued it with a quarter of an inch to spare, and found himself on the way to Chesterford.

The colonel was roaring along between the hedges when the auctioneer's clerk leaned forward and tapped Bill on the shoulder.

"Sergeant," he said, "it is eight-forty-five the bus starts, not seven-forty-five. You had better go back and catch it."

Wagstaff jumped on the brake, and Sergeant Torbin just managed to save the bowl from violent contact with the dashboard. Several of the passengers slid onto the floor, where they continued to sing "Down Mexico Way" half a bar behind the rest.

"So it is!" the colonel exclaimed. "Changed it last week! Well, I'll teach 'em to monkey with the timetable."

And he let in the clutch, cursed the gears, found top and put his foot down.

Bill was still wondering whether the auctioneer's clerk was sober or whether his liquor just made him more clerkly, when the man leaned forward again and tapped the colonel. "Has it occurred to you, sir," he suggested precisely, "that it might be thought you had stolen a corporation bus?"

Sergeant Torbin cuddled the bowl, and this time only bumped his elbow.

"We'll get out here, chaps," the colonel said, pulling up so close to the hedge that they couldn't and had to get out by the driver's door — all except the boatbuilder's foreman, who broke the glass over the emergency exit and managed to make it work. "The Bull is just up the road."

The Bull was a small riverside pub, empty except for two farm hands and a ferryman. It fulfilled, far better than The Greyhound, all Bill's expectations of the quiet English inn.

"Mr. Baker and gentlemen," Wagstaff announced from the head of the procession, "we are celebrating the acquisition of a Greek drinking bowl. Could we allow it to go to America? Never!"

"Say, why not?" Bill asked.

"Because they don't drink wine in America. They drink gin."

Bill was about to say that it was not true, and that works of art were appreciated a darn sight more than . . . but he was too late.

"What's wrong with filling her up with gin?" asked the boatbuilder's foreman.

"Neat?" protested Mr. Baker.

"It is indeed long," said the colonel, "since she was accustomed to those heights of felicity where you, Mr. Baker, would be legally bound to refuse to serve us. So slowly, slowly. Gin and tonic. Half and half. Old Greek custom. Always put water with it. Not the men we are today."

And he began to sing "Land of Our Fathers" at the top of his voice.

Mr. Baker had just filled the bowl when Torbin's ear, trained by conversation in the presence of jet engines, heard the bus draw up outside. He shouted the news at Wagstaff.

The colonel sprang into action.

"Right, Bill! Our fault! Won't get you mixed up in it!"

He pushed the sergeant onto the window seat, made him lie down and covered his uniform with a couple of overcoats. When the bus driver, accompanied by a full load of cops from a police car, crashed through the door, he was kneeling at Bill's side and bathing his forehead with gin and tonic out of the bowl.

"Now which of you gentlemen . . ." a policeman began.

The colonel kept his handkerchief firmly over Bill's mouth

and explained in a voice which was the very perfection of quiet respectability that he had bought a priceless Athenian cylix at the late vicar's late niece's auction, and that an American art dealer had endeavored to steal it from him outside The Greyhound.

Foiled by these gallant citizens and especially by this poor fellow — he tenderly mopped Bill's forehead with gin — the art dealer had made his escape in a corporation bus. They followed, some on foot, some clinging to the vehicle. The bus stopped suddenly just down the road, and the fellow bolted into the darkness before they could get hold of him.

"There was a tall, dark American sergeant in Falkstead this afternoon," said another cop.

They all swore that it wasn't the sergeant. No, a civilian. A little, fairish chap.

"And six of you couldn't stop him?"

"He had a gun," said the boatbuilder's foreman, and choked into his handkerchief.

The bus driver, having no official duty to believe unanimous witnesses, went straight to the point which interested him.

"Which of you blokes broke the window above the emergency door?"

"I did," answered the colonel magnificently. "It was an emergency."

Mr. Baker polished glasses and said nothing. The ferryman and two farm hands waited patiently for free drinks. After telephoning a description of the art dealer to county headquarters, the police escorted the bus back to Falkstead.

"Now, Bill," said the colonel, "be reasonable! Whatever is the use of having allies if one can't put the blame on them?"

"Hell!" Bill replied, and accidentally kicked over the bowl which was on the floor at his feet.

He picked it up and glared protectively at the lot of them.

"Bill, you have upset these gentlemen's liquor."

Sergeant Torbin was in honor bound to have her filled up again. He discovered that he was delighted to do so, and reminded his conscience that the Athenian potter must have designed his wares to stand up to an evening's amusement.

What with one of them pointing out that the horses at the bottom seemed to trot whenever the tonic water fizzed onto the gin, and another swearing it was possible to hold a full bowl by one handle without spilling any — which it wasn't — the strength of the cylix was certainly astonishing. Mr. Baker put the auctioneer's clerk to bed upstairs — explaining that he didn't want his house to get a bad name by turning him loose in the road — and that left Bill aware that he was the only member of the party with any worry at all in the back of his mind. Not that he hadn't been drinking his share. But in the earlier party at The Greyhound, when the rest of them had been laying a foundation of Burgundy as if it were beer, he was too overcome by his respect for the bowl to commit more than a reverent sip whenever it came round to him.

At nine-thirty he suggested that he ought to telephone for a taxi.

"Don't you bother!" the colonel said. "We'll cross the

ferry here, and then it's only half a mile to the junction. He'll get a train from there, won't he, Mr. Baker?"

Mr. Baker consulted a sheet behind the bar, and said pointedly that if he hurried, he would.

They all piled out onto the landing stage, and Mr. Baker locked up the bar, though there was half an hour to go before closing time. The ferryman unchained his punt, and twice took Bill and the colonel nearly over to the other side. The first time he turned round in midstream without noticing it, and the second time he had to put back because the boatbuilder's foreman had fallen off the jetty while waving good-by.

Bill and Colonel Wagstaff landed and set off along the creekside path in single file — until, that is, Bill noticed that Wagstaff had left the bowl behind in the punt.

"Now, see here, Colonel," Bill recommended when they had recovered it, "you let me carry that!"

"O.K.," said the colonel. "Catch!"

After quarter of a mile, Wagstaff, who was leading, sat down on a tussock of grass and began to laugh.

"Bill — guineas!"

Bill grunted. He had reached the sentimental stage of liquor, and his eyes were dramatically wet as soon as he was reminded that for a dollar and a half and a little courage he could have saved a priceless possession from the inevitable smash.

"Not fair! I knew guineas would fox you. Unsporting to take advantage of an ally. Funny at the time, yes! Bill, I present you with the bowl."

"No, Colonel, I won't take her."

"Got to take her."

"Say, we've had a lot to drink, and . . ."

"Boy, I was a military attaché in Moscow."

"Well, that sure makes a difference, Colonel, but . . ."

It did. By the standards of his experience, Bill could not describe the colonel as drunk. He was merely incalculable.

"Also," said Wagstaff repentantly, "I have used it as a common utensil."

"Not yet," Bill answered. "I guess you would if I wasn't carrying it."

"But from now on it is yours."

"Then you let me pay for it," said Bill, handing the bowl to the colonel and feeling for his wallet.

"Not allowed to pay for it. That's an order from a superior officer. Even in retirement, Sergeant, certain privileges attach themselves to . . ."

"Order, my foot!"

"If you won't take it, I'll pitch the bloody thing in the river."

"Go on! You pitch it!"

The colonel did, with a neat backhanded action of the wrist. The cylix flew like a discus into the darkness and landed with a plop on the tidal mud.

Bill Torbin, after one horrified stare at the personified obstinacy of the English, drunk or sober, plunged after it. He squelched out towards the water, while the smell of primeval slime rose from the pits where his legs had been.

The sounds of progress became less violent. There was silence, except for the shunting of a distant train.

"Colonel, I'm stuck," Bill said.

"Nothing to bother about, boy! We're used to it round these parts. Lie on your stomach!"

"I can't. I'm up to my chest."

"Hard underfoot?"

"I wouldn't be talking to you if it wasn't."

"Then I'll come and pull you out."

The colonel advanced over his knees and took off his coat. Keeping hold of one sleeve, he swung the other over to Bill. Between cuff and cuff were a good eight feet.

"I think I see her," Bill said. "You pull me clear and then I'll sort of swim."

Wagstaff pulled. The sergeant emerged as far as the thighs, and flung himself forward down the slope. The object was an old white-enameled basin with a hole in it.

Bill managed to turn, and floundered back like a stranded porpoise until the choice between sinking head first or feet first became urgent. The colonel took a step forward and flung the coat again. He, too, went in up to his chest.

"I guess this mud is covered at high water," Bill said after a pause.

"Float a battleship!" Wagstaff agreed cheerfully. "But there's an hour in the ebb still. Nothing to worry about. Round here everybody knows where everybody is."

"Well, if you say so, Colonel."

"If I'm not home when the pubs shut," Wagstaff explained, "my housekeeper will telephone The Greyhound, because she was expecting me home to dinner. Mr. Watson will telephone Mr. Baker. Mr. Baker will telephone the junction. The stationmaster will say we never arrived, and somebody will come and look for us. You'll see. Cold, this mud, isn't it?"

The comment struck Sergeant Torbin's mixed drinks as excessively funny. He began to hoot with laughter. The colonel, after two or three staccato explosions like an ancient truck protesting against the starting handle, warmed up and joined the racket an octave lower.

"But you shouldn't . . . you shouldn't . . ." yelled Torbin, trying to control himself, "you shouldn't have drunk out of her."

"Only pity for her, Bill. Only pity for her. How would you like to spend sev-seventy years on the vicar's mantelpiece remembering Alci-bibi-biades?"

Bill pulled himself together, mourning perfection farther out on the mud.

"She was safer there," he said solemnly.

"At the mercy of any passing housemaid. Euphemia, she was called. I knew her well. But out of this nettle, safety, we pluck . . ."

"You've got it wrong."

"Shakespeare, Bill."

"Common heritage, Colonel."

"What I mean to say is that when we pick it up it's yours."

"Can't get at ten guineas. Under the mud."

"Then that's settled. Do you know any songs to pass the time, Bill?"

"If I had my ukulele . . ."

"I'll do that bit," said the colonel, "if you don't mind it being a banjo."

Bill's repertoire was good for an hour and a half.

"I could do with a drink," Wagstaff said, giving a final plunk to his imaginary strings.

"That search party is sure taking a long time, Colonel."

"Must have slipped up somewhere. You'd have thought they would have heard us."

"Your turn now."

"I was considering that question in the intervals," Wagstaff said. "The trouble is, Bill, that the only songs I can ever remember were acquired during the sheltered life of school and university, and are of such monstrous indecency that even sergeants' singsongs have been closed to me."

After an hour of the colonel, Bill agreed that the sergeants might be right, and added that he thought the tide was rising.

"Eight hours down, and four hours up," said Wagstaff.

"Not six?"

"Four."

"Hadn't we better try to get out?"

"You can try, Bill."

After ten minutes Bill said:

"I guess I'll learn some of those songs of yours, Colonel, when I've got my breath back."

"Repeat the words after me, Bill, facing the land."

In competition with each other, they so concentrated upon the job in hand that neither heard the approaching craft until she was three hundred yards away. With the fast tide under her, she was abreast of them before their yells for help met with any response.

" 'Old on!" shouted the bridge. "It ain't easy, yer know!"

The engine-room telegraph rang. The wash from the pro-peller slid up the mudbank as the ship was held steady in the tide. A beam of light glared into their faces.

The captain certainly knew his channel well. Going gently astern, he edged into the bank until the bows towered above them. Prettily riding the crest of a wavelet, right under the forefoot of the ship, was the bowl.

"Look out!" Bill shouted. "You'll run her down."

"Never saw there was another of you!" bawled the captain.

The telegraph rang violently. White water swirled at the stern. Their rescuer withdrew, edging out a little into the current, and the tide promptly swung the ship in a quarter circle with the bows as center. The captain went ahead in a desperate effort to regain steerage way, and there she was, aground fore and aft across the channel.

"Knew that would 'appen," said the captain, addressing them conversationally from the forecastle. "Now where's the lady?"

"No lady," the colonel replied. "She walked home."

"What? And left you there?"

"Must have forgotten."

"Cor! What I'd 'ave said if I'd known there was no lady! Well, catch 'old!"

The rope fell by Wagstaff. The captain, the mate and the one deck hand dragged him, wallowing, through the mud and up the side of the ship.

Sergeant Torbin followed, but left the rope in order to

plunge sideways and recover the bowl. By the time the mate had recoiled the line and flung it back, very little sergeant was visible beyond his cap and an outstretched arm.

"What d'yer do that for?" asked the captain, when Bill too was safe on board. "Balmy?"

"It's two thousand years old," Bill explained.

"Like me frying pan," said the mate. "Went up to me waist for that one, I did. Fifty year old it might be, and they don't make 'em like that no more."

The captain led the way to a small saloon under the bridge. It reeked of fug and decayed vegetables but was gloriously warm.

"You take them things off, and Bert will 'ang 'em in the engine room," he said.

"Any old clothes will do," the colonel invited, dropping coat and trousers in a solid lump on the floor.

"Ain't got none. Don't keep a change on board, not none of us."

"Blanket will do."

"Don't sleep on board neither."

"What are you?" the colonel asked.

"Chesterford garbage scow. Takes it from the trucks and dumps it overboard at forty fathom, see? Never out at night, we aren't, unless we misses a tide like we done yesterday. Bert, give 'em a couple of towels and shovel up them clothes!"

Bill managed to make the towel meet round his waist. The colonel found his wholly inadequate.

"I'll try this," said Wagstaff cheerfully, lifting the bowl

from the cabin table and removing the tablecloth. "Show you how they wear 'em in India!"

The cloth had once been red plush, but the pile was smooth with age and grease stains. The colonel folded it diagonally, passed two corners through his legs, knotted the tassels and beamed on the captain.

"Well, I suppose," said the captain grudgingly, "that you'd both better 'ave a drop of rum, though it don't look to me as if it was so long since the last one."

He unlocked a first-aid cabinet and produced a bottle.

"I admit with pride that we have been celebrating the acquisition of a priceless antique," the colonel answered.

"This 'ere?"

"That there."

"Sort of basin, like?"

"An old Greek drinking bowl, Captain."

"How's it used?"

"It was *not* used," the sergeant shouted. "They kept it to look at. On the mantelpiece."

"Nonsense, Bill! They didn't have mantelpieces. I'll show you, Captain. A slave took the jug, so!" The colonel seized the bottle of rum. "And emptied it into the bowl, so!"

"Hey!" the skipper protested.

"And then it went round like a loving cup."

Wagstaff took a sip and with both hands passed the bowl courteously to the captain, who could only drink and pass it on to Bill. Bill despairingly lowered the level by quarter of an inch, gasped and passed it to the mate — the mate to Bert.

"Good navy rum, that!" said the colonel, starting the bowl on its round again.

"Got to stay where we are for the time being," the mate agreed. "Bert, you take them clothes away like the skipper ordered, and then you can 'ave a lie-down."

With the memory of the rising tide safely behind him, Bill felt that there was some excuse for the theory that an object should be used as its maker intended. Half an hour later, inspired by his towel, he was showing them a dance he had learned in the South Pacific, when he began to think the saloon was going round.

It was. The stern of the garbage scow, gently lifted from the mud, swung across river with increasing speed and thudded into the opposite bank. Bill made a dive for the bowl as it slid across the table and landed in the captain's lap.

"Knew that would 'appen!" the skipper yelled. "That's the last time I picks a Yank out of the mud!"

He jammed in the doorway with the mate. The bows came off the mud and described the same semicircle as the stern. The engine-room telegraph rang like a fire engine. Wagstaff, flung off the settee onto the floor, sat there cross-legged, shaking with laughter. Bill cradled the bowl grimly on his knees.

"Allies, Bill, allies! What did I tell you? It's all your fault, and your towel has come off!"

"Colonel," said Bill, reknotting it round his waist, "how come all the guys that tried to shoot you missed?"

He dropped his head on the table, and instantly fell asleep.

They were awakened by Bert, flinging down two still-soggy bundles of clothes.

"Skipper says 'e don't want no more to do with either of you," he announced, "and if you ain't off this scow as soon as we ties up 'e'll send for the police."

It was light. Up the reach the town, the castle and the municipal rubbish dump of Chesterford were in sight. The clock on the church tower made the time eight-thirty.

"Bill," said Wagstaff, breaking the silence, "that piece of linen in which you have wrapped the bowl was once my shirt."

"Say, Colonel, I'm sorry. I wasn't thinking."

"Not a word. It will dry there. And I can do up my coat collar. Thank heaven I am known in Chesterford!"

Bill took the remark on trust, though it seemed to him when he was escorted by the mate through the corrugated iron door of the garbage wharf, before breakfast and looking as if he had been dug out of the tip, that personally he would prefer a town where he was not known.

Striding up the main street of Chesterford, however, alongside the colonel, he understood. Wagstaff's air was guiltless, so full indeed of a casual manliness as he greeted an occasional acquaintance that only one of them thought it proper to comment on his appearance.

"Showing our friend here some sport," said the colonel. "Mallard right. Teal left. Got 'em both. Lost me balance. And this gallant fellow hauled me out."

As they resumed their squelching progress up the High Street, Bill remarked that he had sounded exactly like a British colonel in the movies.

"A very useful accomplishment," Wagstaff agreed, "which has enabled me before now to rescue allies from well-deserved court-martial. Later in the day which is now upon us, Bill, or even tomorrow or whenever that damned bowl permits us both a reasonably sober countenance, I shall accompany you to your commanding officer and obtain for you a mention in your home-town paper and probably a medal from the Royal Humane Society."

"What's that?"

"It gives medals. Did you not leap into mud of unknown bottom to rescue me?"

"Don't mention it, Colonel. It was the least I could do," said Bill, and paused. "Say, wasn't it the bowl?"

"The values are quite irrelevant, Bill. Me or the bowl? The bowl or me? We will now go into The Red Lion here for a bath and breakfast."

"Will the bar be open yet, Colonel?"

"Oh, that'll be all right. They know me there."

"Then I'm not going in with this bowl," Bill said firmly. "Not to The Red Lion or any other of your animal friends."

"Fresh herrings, Bill. I can smell 'em. And bacon and eggs to follow."

"We can have breakfast at a teashop."

"Too respectable. They wouldn't let us in."

Sergeant Torbin, desperately searching the market square for safety, was inspired by the opening of the double doors of the Chesterford Museum. He ran, vaulted the turnstile in the vestibule, where the doorkeeper was just changing into his uniform coat, and charged down an alley of Roman tombstones into a collection of stuffed foxes and weasels marked NATURAL HISTORY. Hesitating wildly between NEOLITHIC, IRON AGE and GENTLEMEN, he saw a door to his left with CURATOR on it. He leaped through it, and found himself facing a desk where a very tall wisp of a man in his seventies was quietly cataloguing.

"You take this," he said. "Lock it up in your safe, quick!"

Before the curator could get over the shock of an American sergeant covered with mud from head to foot and offering with outstretched arms an unknown object wrapped in dirty linen, Wagstaff also was upon him.

"Is it — is it a baby?" the curator asked.

"It is, sir, a fifth-century Attic cylix," the colonel replied with dignity.

The curator tremblingly extracted the bowl, and at the sight of it instantly recovered an almost ecclesiastical self-possession.

"But this is an article of great value," he intoned.

"I know it is. You've no idea of the trouble I've had preserving it from destruction."

"This — um — er — has dispossessed you of it?"

"Lord, no! It's his."

"Colonel, it is yours," said Bill with what he hoped was finality.

The colonel took the bowl with both hands, pledged an imaginary draught to the gods and held it high above the stone floor of the curator's office.

"I've nowhere to keep it!" Bill screamed.

"Oh, that's all that is bothering you, is it?" the colonel exclaimed. "Well, what's that damned owl doing?"

A stuffed barn owl in a Victorian showcase stood on the

curator's workbench. Wagstaff lifted the glass dome from the ebony base and removed the owl, which immediately disintegrated into dust and feathers.

"Moldy," said the colonel. "Disgrace to the museum. That reminds me, I believe I'm on the committee. Give you a new one and stuff it myself."

"I was indeed considering . . ." the curator began.

"Of course you were. Quite right! Mind if I sit down at your desk a minute?"

The colonel printed a neat card:

LENT TO THE MUSEUM BY COURTESY OF
SERGEANT WILLIAM TORBIN, U.S.A.F.

He laid the bowl upon the ebony stand and propped the card up against it.

"That will keep *you* quiet," he said, replacing the glass dome, "until Bill has a mantelpiece for you again. The sergeant has only got to write to you to get it, I suppose?" he added fiercely to the curator.

"Yes, yes, but . . ."

"Any objection to The Red Lion now, Bill? It will be a pleasant change to drink out of glasses once more."

Drug for the Major

HE WAS a severe creature, the Major, seldom smiling, always aloof. How he amused himself — if he ever did — when there was no war, one couldn't imagine. He was a most unlikely person to be a successful leader of partisans in enemy country, for he lacked all the lighter human interests. His men did not love him, but they had to respect him. His patience was as coldly Napoleonic as his manner. Every operation he undertook had been a deliberate, foolproof success.

Brigadier Callender could only hope that this brilliant managing of luck would continue. He wished he were anywhere else in the world but that naked Greek hillside. At the same time there was no denying that this was the very glory and height of boy's book soldiering. His own job was purely administration, but what he administered were all the little British forces operating behind the enemy lines in Greece, Italy and Yugoslavia; and, since he was not the sort of soldier who preferred his facts on paper, he did at times appear in person to those of his charges who could be reached at all. He could do a lot to comfort such individualists, each of them forced by isolation to exaggerate his own private and military problems. He was double the age of most of them.

Sixteen men were waiting in a very slight fold of a hillside so open that anyone could see its emptiness at a glance. They were more or less dressed in British uniform; if captured, they could only hope that the Germans would consider it more, not less. Their presence — since they had taken up their position before dawn — could not possibly be imagined by the enemy post guarding the bridge three hundred feet below, where the rock-cut road leaped from one bank of the gorge to the other. They had waited all day. They were waiting now for the road patrol to pass. They would then blow the bridge and wait again till nightfall to get away.

The Major seemed to have a genius for waiting. There he sat, apart as usual, his back against a rock, drafting what looked like a particularly difficult letter with his leather brief case open on his knees. Ever since Callender had dropped into this little command — descending godlike upon Mount Olympus — and found himself helplessly committed to an operation for which it was already on the move, he had never seen the Major without his brief case. It was slung on his hip together with his maps, inseparable from his person as if it contained the most secret documents in the whole Middle East.

Tactful questioning had not produced the slightest evidence of what it did contain. His own very personal bottle of tablets perhaps? Well, provided he knew how to use them, there was no great harm in that. They could all have done with any secret stimulant or bromide — according to temperament — which was going. The brief case seemed at any rate to supply for the Major that escape from unpleasantly real reality which men less self-sufficient might have found in a book or a game of chess.

Callender looked over his companions in the hollow. All but the Major were on edge, some fidgety, some unnaturally tense. Three were silently playing cards, with olive stones for chips. The second-in-command was trying to write home and making a poor job of it. The simpler and more blessed were asleep, but twitching. One or two were trying to read what they already knew by heart. The sergeant-major was carving a recognizable donkey out of a mandrake root.

The silence of autumn afternoon sang through the mountains and resolved itself into the rattle of a tracked vehicle and the whine of trucks in bottom gear. That, presumably, was the road patrol. No one moved. Only the Major rolled over to the skyline and had a look at the enemy. The patrol halted, then rumbled on over the bridge and up the pass. The Major returned impassively to his correspondence.

After half an hour he put his papers back in the brief case and locked it. This simple action, methodical as that of any businessman arriving at his suburban station, seemed to be a recognized signal. Books were pocketed. The sleepers awoke. Cards were returned to a haversack, olive stones swept into a cigarette tin.

In single file the commando crawled down the sheltering fold until they were within seventy yards of the enemy post and cover was no more than the foot-high brush of the hillside. The operation was astonishingly swift and efficient — almost, Callender thought, humane. Not one of the eight Germans guarding the bridge was wounded. Their post was scientifically planned. Their defense was tactically correct and predictable. Consequently they were all dead.

The charges took eighteen and a half minutes to lay. Then there was no bridge, and the road itself was safe only for foot passengers. The Major's faith in his sources of information was justified, for such traffic as interrupted the operation — and hastily cleared off — was civilian and apologetic.

Before the dust wholly settled, the commando had vanished into that inadequate hollow and resumed its former occupations. Callender found the second period of waiting intolerable. The road below, on both sides of the gorge, began to hum with enemy activity; and what was happening in the valleys across which they had to withdraw he could, as a soldier, imagine. Only the Major knew if the chance of the sixteen to return to the mountain cave which they called headquarters was really as good as he insisted it was.

The Brigadier reminded himself that patience had been the essence of soldiering since the siege of Troy. Looking back through his memories of an infantry subaltern in 1916, he found them dominated by the periods of waiting. Action was a mere flash of blinding light dividing the endless mists of doing nothing. But at least, in those days, they had known what was in front of them and what behind. These chaps didn't. Yet they waited till their plan was perfected; waited, at the mercy of a cough, for the moment of action; waited again for the chance to escape. And all this behind the enemy lines.

He longed as never in his life for a cigarette, which of course was forbidden. The readers of books could not keep their attention fixed. The cardplayers went through the motions of enthusiasm, but the deals grew slower until they were finally abandoned. Only the Major was imperturbable. Out came the brief case, now white with stone dust from the bridge, and to work he went. He tore up what he had written before the action and started again.

Surely the man, unapproachable as he was, would permit the congratulations of a senior officer? Callender crawled over to him, stopped tactfully, and was beckoned on.

"If only," said the Major in a savage whisper, "I could do that to GHQ!"

He jerked a thumb in the direction of the bridgeless gorge.

"Your wish is shared by quite half the Army," the Brigadier answered mildly. "Generally for the wrong reasons."

"*You* people could be a lot worse."

"We try. I know how dense we must seem to you sometimes. But we do try."

The Major's whispered wrath boiled up again.

"By God, you do! Look at the trouble you go to just to get us mail! How's that for administration? And what's the good of it, sir? What's the good of it?"

The exasperated exclamation was odd and revealing. The Major might well have asked what was the good of writing home when you were not allowed to say a word of what you were doing, and what you were seeing or how you lived. But to complain that he could still receive letters! Trouble at home, probably.

Callender made an opening move.

"What did you do in peacetime?"

"Me? Cotton."

The Major's brusque reply called up a picture of some hardheaded North Countryman for whom bales of cotton

had taken the place of human faces. He offered no details of
what he did with his cotton — possibly moved it from hither
to yon with solid accuracy and by unexpected routes. Certainly the quicksilver dealings of merchants and brokers
were not for him.

"Is there anything I can do for you if I — when I — get
back?" the Brigadier asked, trying again.

"Yes. Find out who writes letters marked OOA/117/42/K
and have him dropped in the drink."

Callender recognized OOA as originating from the Pay
Department. That the Major should be annoyed at some
obtuseness in dealing with his pay and allowances was not
surprising.

"I'll look into that, of course." He smiled. "But I meant —
well, more private troubles. For example, if there's anything
which can only be handled by a —" the Major's cold eyes
were embarrassing — "by a personal friend, would it be any
help if I were to ask him to lunch?"

"I'm not married," said the Major bluntly.

A devastating, almost a cynical reply. But to the point.
Nine tenths of army misery were due to helpless inability to
deal with the problems of wife and children. Still, there
were enough other pitiable human complexities. The Major
seemed to ignore them altogether.

At blessed last it was night. The Major led his party over
the ridge and down into the broad, cultivated valley beyond
— very slowly, of course, but without any marked hesitation.
The unseen pattern of fords and field paths ahead of them
did not seem to share the mountain silence, but it was impossible to pinpoint a definite sound.

The second-in-command felt his way from the rear up the single file of unhurried, carefully stepping men.

"I imagine they'll be holding the Ktipito track in force, sir."

"I have no use for imagination," the Major snapped. "I like to know."

The boy was only a shadow on the night, but Callender could see from his cheerful bearing that he did not resent the snub. All of them were accustomed to the Teutonic lack of frivolity in their leader's mind. In a way it was a guarantee for his understanding of the enemy.

"I'm going on until I bump into them," the Major added.

Callender's staff training leaped to his lips in protest. But on second thoughts the Major was right. Reconnoitering was impossible. He could not separate his command or he'd never see half of them again. The fact was that the man had the ideal character for movement in the dark. Night maneuvers would not go wrong if the leader were so unimaginative that he never thought a tree stump was a man, so stolid that he never hesitated as to which of two half-glimpsed tracks was right when he knew perfectly well in daylight which was right.

At the crossing of the main road they did bump into the enemy — if you could call it a bump when you saw him first and merely waited interminably for him to go away. The Major did not even pay him the compliment of lying down. He sat primly with his back against a fig tree. His whole familiar attitude suggested that if there had been light for writing he would have opened his brief case. That his mind worked on the correspondence was certain.

When movement was safe and road crossed, the ground began to rise and again there was stone underfoot. The enemy was not so silent, not so sure as they that darkness was an ally. The Major, leading, bumped in person. His commando knife — which Callender so disliked on indents for its air of flamboyant self-consciousness — was effective. So was the drill, even to the catching of the lieutenant's body as he fell. He was elderly. He should not have turned out so conscientiously for this kind of duty. He should not have visited his posts alone.

The Brigadier never knew what else they passed on the Ktipito track. He doubted if any of them did. But the point which mattered was that whatever existed outside the twenty-yard range of their exceptional night sight *had* been passed — and the Major, on any less familiar route, could never have been sure of that.

At dawn they were among the high rocks where even Greeks did not try to scratch the pockets of soil and even the angriest of German commanders could perceive that search for them would be fruitless. A Greek guide and a mule were there already. The guide had laid out the rations and wine as if for a picnic. He had astonishingly provided a white tablecloth. It was his personal gesture of hospitality.

"I'll send you back with him after breakfast," the Major said to Callender. "We shall wait."

Waiting again? How could he endure it? And it wasn't just for rest. The night march, though it included some tough climbing, had been welcome even to the middle-aged Callender after the interminable motionless hours. No, that Napoleonic Major had decided to wait a day or two just to find out what steps the enemy had in fact taken, just to avoid guesswork and impatience if ever they undertook a second operation in those valleys.

After breakfast some slept, some smoked. The Major, of course, did not smoke. He took out his brief case, scrubbed off as well as might be a dark stain on the leather and set to work.

"I can take the mail," Callender offered.

"It's all ready for you at our headquarters."

"Nothing urgent — here?"

"Urgent?" the Major barked, the harshness of strain in his exasperated voice. "No, nothing urgent!"

He hauled a pile of official correspondence from that precious brief case and slammed it on the baked ground in front of Callender.

The Brigadier noticed that the case was left empty. There was no bottle of tablets. Not even a photograph. Not even a letter in a woman's handwriting.

"That's all?" he asked, in spite of himself.

"All? Good God, the bloody file's an inch thick!"

It was. Neatly pinned together and indexed were carbon copies of the Major's penciled letters to the Pay Department and their formal replies.

"They owe me twenty-nine pounds, seventeen shillings," said the Major, "and I am *going* to get it."

The gist of the correspondence was clear at once to Callender's practiced eye. Twenty-nine pounds, seventeen shillings had been knocked off the Major's pay for the simple bureaucratic reason that he had spent the money and not accounted for it. Nobody, however, expected the details of expenditure from secret funds to be precisely entered. The Major had merely to write out a voucher, sign it and get it countersigned by his commanding officer.

But that was not the Major's style. He derided the Pay Department. He parodied their formalities and their references. His bitter incoherence was such that OOA/117/42/K had himself become affected and caught the ungraciousness of his correspondent.

"You see, sir! All my spare time taken up writing to those . . ."

The Major let loose upon the Pay a string of oaths so sincere that they had the sting of ecclesiastical curses. Callender vaguely perceived that they were directed to the wrong address. The Pay was eminently cursable. It wasn't much good to curse the enemy or the brutality of killing or the never-ending responsibility for the lives of sixteen men and a host of civilian helpers.

OOA/117/42/K did partly deserve the fury which he had invoked. He had allowed himself to lose sight of the point, and the result was complicated verbiage. Callender, when he returned to his office, could straighten out the Major's problem in three minutes on the telephone.

He was about to say so, opened his mouth — and shut it. It would be cruelly unintelligent to deprive the Major of his grievance. If the drafting, the filing, the absurd indexing of this correspondence were ended, what recreation would be left, to support the tormented hours of waiting, for a man who took no pleasure in his fellows or himself, wouldn't talk and didn't read?

"There is no way for me to interfere in a financial matter of this sort," he said gently. "But they'll see sense in the end if you go on trying to settle it yourself by letter."

As Best He Can

"WE ARE safe here, Dominique?"

"Quite safe, *mon commandant*. The Boches never move outside their camp at night. Why should they? Our women are loyal. And there is nothing else to do in these sand dunes."

"All the same, you're taking a risk with that light."

"It cannot be seen. We are down in a hollow, and my pickets are out all round us."

"And no Boches on the beach?"

"They are forbidden to walk on the beach after dark. It might not be healthy."

"But the relations of your district with the camp are correct?"

"Quite correct, *mon commandant*. If anything happens, we are careful that it should appear an accident. The Boches have altogether forgotten that we are Frenchmen."

"They find too many collaborators."

"Some. It's inevitable. But all are harmless, except this prisoner with whom I wish the court to deal. He could betray us if he wished."

"It is a question of the death sentence?"

"That is for the court to decide, *mon commandant*. Hith-

erto Dumetrier has refused to give any explanation of his behavior."

"I see. Well, Dominique, my colleagues and I are ready if
you will bring him before us. . . . But he's a fine-looking
type! . . . One would be sure of getting a decent bottle at
his establishment. . . . Your name?"

"Louis Alphonse Dumetrier. And yours?"

"You may address me as the President of the Court."

"Very well, M. le Président."

"Your occupation?"

"Café proprietor."

"Have you any objection to the court?"

"Not the slightest, M. le Président — except that it is held
in the middle of the night when a businessman like myself
should be asleep."

"You can be put to sleep for a very long time, *mon
vieux.*"

"In that case may I request you to see that they do not
make a mess of it as they did when poor Charles Yonne had
an accident with his gun in passing through a hedge?"

"You are well informed, Dumetrier."

"A café proprietor overhears much, M. le Président."

"Therefore his loyalty must be beyond question."

"Agreed, M. le Président. But when a man has a wife and
children his loyalty should not be too obviously beyond
question."

"Do you think then that we of the Resistance have not
wives and children?"

"There is no need for excitement. Each of us serves as
best he can."

"Dumetrier, it is not service to rescue enemy soldiers from the sea. M. Dominique, whose position in the Resistance you unfortunately know, demands an investigation of your motives."

"I doubt if M. Dominique has closely regarded the circumstances, M. le Président."

"Very well. We know the difficulties of Frenchmen, and you will not find the court unsympathetic. Tell us a little of your life."

"What is there to tell? In the summer, before the war I made what I could from holiday visitors. For the rest of the year, there were the regular clients — a few farmers, a few fishermen. And on fine Sundays in spring and autumn there would be parties for lunch."

"And now?"

"Well, M. le Président, as M. Dominique will have told you, I am on excellent terms with the Boches. And as I usually have a few delicacies from their army rations, it makes life easier for us all."

"That is because you make a habit of trying to save them from drowning?"

"Hardly a habit, M. le Président. There were only three. And a little effort impresses the Boches."

"Before the war you were commended for gallantry in saving life, I believe?"

"There was no damned gallantry! It's all a farce for a man who knows the beach as I do. Look, M. le Président, our beach is safe for children who never venture out beyond the breakers, and safe for a strong swimmer who is not afraid of the current and knows how to ride his way in on top of the waves. But for young people who have been trained in swimming baths and think they know it all — there is the danger!"

"There have been fatalities?"

"Fewer than you would think. One is always on the watch. I am no Channel swimmer, M. le Président, but I know the breakers and, without exaggeration, I can do in the water what I wish."

"So the court understands. But what is incredible, Dumetrier, is that you should treat the enemy as if they were young Frenchmen on holiday. Listen to me! Do not shrug your shoulders! France is occupied, and it is no time for humanity."

"Humanity does not specially interest me, M. le Président."

"What then? What then? Do you deny that on three separate occasions you have risked your life to rescue German soldiers? You do not think of your wife and children then, scum of a collaborator!"

"No. When it is a question of Germans I do not think of my wife and children."

"But it is unbelievable! This animal prefers to his family some damned Boches who are in difficulties and have not the strength to get back to shore!"

"I do not know whether they had the strength or not, M. le Président. When strong swimmers are waiting for a wave to bring them in, it is very hard to see from the beach if they are really in trouble."

"But you were ready to assume they were!"

"Oh, yes, I always assumed they were."

"And was it necessary to save them?"

"I do not think it was always necessary."

"And yet you admit risking your life to bring them in!"

"M. le Président, I admit I brought them in. But they were none of them alive when we reached the shore."

Moment of Truth

SHE begged me for it. You know how divinely exalted young women can become. Begged for a cyanide pill as though it were her right, as though I should be doing her out of a great spiritual experience if I hesitated. Men don't behave like that at all. A man accepts the means of death without looking at it, hides it in his smallest pocket and examines it with loathing when he gets home or wherever is serving him as a home. No, martyrdom for us has no attraction — not, at any rate, for the more active type.

You never dreamed she had that sort of past, did you? And I would not have told you, if you hadn't made that unjust remark about her: bright and beautiful as the vicar's daughter in a Victorian novel. Pah!

There's nothing artificial in her character. It's not an attack of poise brought on by reading too many women's magazines. Dina impresses everyone, even on first acquaintance, with her extraordinary inner happiness. It's real, and only an unromantic mind like yours could have thought it was not. She adores her husband. Can't see anything ordinary in him. And she is convinced that there were never such children as hers. Nothing exceptional in that, of course — except that she happens to be right. Dina is entirely without any sense of guilt — that unnecessary, unjustified sense of guilt which takes the spirit out of so many of our highly civilized women. She is in love with life and she can't forget it.

I suppose you know that Dina is of pure Polish blood and breeding. By 1944 there was nothing left, of all she believed in, but patriotism. War and politics had made her an orphan, and the little legacy which would have taken her through the university was reduced to nothing. So when she was about to become a charge on public funds she was shipped off from Warsaw as a foreign worker, and found herself in a factory at Düsseldorf making sights for guns. The Germans are a most extraordinary people. Can you imagine any other nation filling up their country with enemies in wartime? They couldn't believe that Europe really disliked being conquered by nice, comfortable, honest Nazis.

In Dina's factory I was a very favored person, working on special lenses. That's a job which trains a man to infinite patience and readiness to accept disappointment. It married in with my real interest, which was to interfere in every way open to me — very minor ways — with the production of munitions. I was not suspected. The whole of my political past in Austria made me a very probable Nazi sympathizer. My reason for loathing Hitler and all that he stood for was simply good taste. That's a motive quite outside the ken of policemen, and I didn't go out of my way to explain it.

Dina was reported to me as promising material. Among so many worn, shabby, still-pretty girls she was inconspicuous, but she had the advantage that even in the rain and smoke of Düsseldorf you could always spot her, if you were looking for her, a long way off. I had her watched for six months before I employed her.

I became fonder of her — in a fatherly way — than was strictly professional. She was so graceful and slight, with a corona of fair, fine curls and big brown eyes burning to shake the world, or at any rate that part of it governed by Hitler. And so very, very young. If she had been born ten years later than she was, all that emotion — well, it might have found an outlet in crazy worship of some crooner or other. As it was, she had as single a mind as a tiger cub on its first kill without the help of mother.

I had not the heart to use her for much except messages; and once or twice, when it was reasonably safe, she accidentally left a little parcel of explosives — disguised as a packet of sandwiches, for example — in contact with a machine lathe. She had little to fear from any ordinary questioning. She could readily admit that she ran innocent errands for me.

The less one knew, the better. But I had occasionally to deliver material to another organization — a suicidal outfit of Poles, led by a Colonel Lipski who passed himself off as a sturdy blacksmith from Posen. Communication with him was difficult — we were taking our orders from different sources — and I had recourse to Dina. She could disappear into the wet, black streets and become part of the drifting smoke and drifting masses. It was quite natural for Poles to forgather. We all had so much freedom.

That's an odd view of wartime Germany, isn't it? But sometimes, after working hours, the streets seemed to hold more foreigners than Germans. The situation must have been a nightmare for the Gestapo. They did their best. Efficiency was impossible, so they made up for it by terror. In our factory alone they tortured and shot four men for sabotage. Two were loyal Nazis. One was their own agent. And the fourth, a very conscientious foreman. A little too conscientious. In that fog of suspicion we were remarkably successful at faking evidence against anyone who was better dead.

Still, human nature was on the Gestapo side. Their agents, sharing a street corner or a café or just a damp patch of shadow with weary foreigners, were bound to make friends. Those war slaves were simple people, straight from tenements or villages. Five per cent would betray whatever they didn't understand for money; and twenty per cent couldn't keep a secret without telling a neighbor. That made a full quarter whom it was lethal to trust. And into that sullen, formless mass I had to send Dina. She must have felt a little like your Victorian vicar's daughter then.

Some such murderous rumor, something whispered and overheard in the dusk at the factory gate, enveloped Lipski and his organization. I don't suppose the Gestapo knew at first what would come out of the arrests. But Dina and I knew. Lipski hated too passionately. If they really went to work on him, he was likely to spit in his interrogator's face and boast of his past and what he had done — naturally taking all the blame on himself. He was a very gallant man, but not clever. A trained Gestapo expert, with such a spirited confession to work from, could lead the blacksmith-colonel much farther along his line of contacts than he ever meant to go.

It was then that Dina came to my workshop. She had every right to be there. She was employed in the storekeeper's office, and I used to pass my indents through her.

My assistants just grinned whenever I invited her into my little private office. Not unpleasantly. The smiles merely commented on the sentiment of a middle-aged Austrian for a waif as tense as the glass on which he worked.

"I shall be next," she said.

She gloried in it. Think of your own daughter in her most unaccountable and resolute mood — that was Dina! She might have determined to run away and get married. A grim bridegroom. Not to be feared if he embraced her instantaneously. But the Gestapo might ensure that the honeymoon was protracted.

It was a wonder that she had not been arrested already. Lipski was possibly unconscious for the time being.

"Try to believe that you know nothing," I told her. "Why shouldn't you have taken messages for me? My assistants, the foreman, the office boy — they are always trotting about the works with notes from me. I have a passion for writing notes. Forget down to the bottom of your soul that what I gave you had any more significance than what I give them!"

She refused to be put off.

"It's not the messages among ourselves," she answered. "I am the only person who could lead the police from Lipski to us."

"But you will not," I assured her.

"How can you know I won't?" she cried. "How can *I* know? We must make sure — both of us."

I pretended not to know what she wanted. She was so young, and death is so irrevocable.

"You promised," she said.

Well, I had — to all of them who worked directly under me. Yes, I had explained to them that instant death was quite painless, reminded them that soldiers seldom had that much luck, told them that the only thing to fear was betrayal of a comrade. All very suitable. No doubt there were thousands of commanding officers handing out the same line on both sides of twenty different fronts. But that did not make it less true.

I had the pills locked up with my personal instruments, marked ASPIRIN. Hold one in your handkerchief, male or female, convey it to your mouth and crunch. A remedy that no one should be without, as the advertisements say. It was a pity that the establishment behind Lipski had never distributed free samples. But they were doing sabotage on a shoestring.

Dina was bound to be questioned. Lipski would not give her away — not even spitting at them. Poles are always chivalrous. But nothing could prevent them from finding out, by a process of elimination, that she was among three or four suspects who came into the story out of darkness and vanished back into darkness. And Dina, of course, could lead them to me. Not that I mattered. I had cyanide, too.

I gave her what the situation demanded, remembering — oh, what she was alive and all she wouldn't be if she were dead.

Dina was arrested next day. She did her duty. Only eighteen she was when her teeth met in the pill. Don't they say that all his past life revolves before a drowning man? Well, before her, in the second that was left to her, revolved all the future she might have had. The lovers, the husband, the children, the peace which somehow, someday, would bring long, unimaginable years.

Less than a second, I had told her. But there was time in it for a moment of truth when the fifty or sixty years which might have been could advance her, on account, their visions of fulfillment.

Just as real, perhaps, as a glimpse of heaven to the old and pious. But she was too young. No harps or angels or Nirvana for her. Life — that was the heaven which Dina saw unfolding. Yet she crunched and she swallowed, and her heart raced so that she thought its last fluttering was on her. But still the heavy boots marched on each side of her, and she with them.

All men are much the same. My duty was to see that she died before she could talk. Theirs was to exterminate the saboteur. Yet they were quite content to question her decently for a day, and then put her in Ravensbrück Camp as a highly suspicious character against whom nothing definite could be proved. Even in Ravensbrück the commandant made a sort of pet of her. When for a few seconds you have longed to live with a passion that most of us never know in our whole existence, your joy thereafter is bound to make its mark on those around you.

And so on to this day. What we see in her is a woman whose every cell is still rejoicing because it is alive. There's little room for hurt after a rebirth like that, and none at all for guilt. And love of husband and children is an unexpected gift of God that goes far beyond the hackneyed phrase, even beyond her dreams of them while crunching cyanide. That is the explanation of Dina.

A miracle? No. I gave her real aspirin, of course. There are times when the preservation of an individual is more important than any good reason of state. Isn't that what we were fighting about?

Salute

MADAME Clémence was in her neat office at the back of the shop. She did not enjoy selling. Her prosperity depended upon a flair for buying and her own adventurous taste. She trusted to the little window which overlooked the silver-white counters and the blue carpet to enable her to keep an eye on the tastes and nationalities of her customers.

Waiting to be served was a tall woman, elegantly Swedish or German, who examined the hand-woven silks with a leisurely grace in which was no impatience or indeed the slightest suggestion that patience was demanded. As she looked upwards to follow the stroll of an embroidered mandarin across his willow-pattern bridge, the light fell full upon the strong angles of her face. Clémence exclaimed, and ran down the five steps from her office.

At the bottom, with an impulsive, merry gesture, she flicked the imitation of a French Army salute. The other, instantly recognizing her, responded by a joyous exaggeration of a Prussian officer and then held out both her hands. A ten minutes' conversation, begun fifteen years earlier in the office of the Gestapo at Lille, had been picked up exactly at the point where it left off.

"Madame," said Clémence, "still carries herself like a young countess."

"And you, Madame, have changed in nothing," answered the German.

She spoke good international French with a cool, neutral accent which was as restful to Clémence as the familiar voice of a sister.

"I was just about to leave," the Frenchwoman said. "It would give me great pleasure if Madame were free to lunch with me."

"I should be delighted."

As the two walked down a short, sun-checkered street to the restaurant where Clémence entertained such business acquaintances as cared deeply what they ate, the men who were walking up it turned their heads — in tribute to distinction rather than in hope of response. It was a tribute which neither, if alone, could have been quite certain of receiving. The German was lithe and long-legged with classic features which life and summer suns had dried nearly to severity. Clémence, though she had preserved the leaf-brown hair and cream complexion of her teens, was aware — with as much humor as regret, since she was most happily married — that her figure had begun to share their luxuriance. She was thirty-two, and supposed that the German was about ten years older.

Clémence chose from the menu for her companion's unknown tastes, asking with lifted eyebrow if her guesses were correct and receiving unspoken confirmation. They discussed Paris and — a little — politics. In spite of their strange certainty of friendship, facts compelled reticence. Her guest had been a secretary to the Gestapo.

"This Vouvray is so refreshing, Madame."

"I am enchanted that you like it. Your vines have recovered from the winter of 1956?"

"They are accustomed to the stupidities of our land," answered the German with a smile which was half melancholy, half invitation.

"You were really — just a secretary?"

"Nothing more. I wrote French well, you see. That is not so common."

"All the same," Clémence protested, "when I think of those files . . ."

"They were not as you imagine. Every army must look after its security. Your own *deuxième bureau* would have used controls and records like ours."

"Dear Madame, I do not even know what to call you," said Clémence, noticing the nervous movements of her long fingers.

"Herta. I saw your name for the first time in the shop, Clémence."

"And . . . a family?"

"A widow. He was on the Russian front when I was in France."

"There is nothing else but to serve too — wherever we can."

"Clémence, I knew nothing of the treatment of prisoners. That was the unforgivable horror. But in our office there was no brutality. We had no cells. We were only investigating commercial offenses."

The Frenchwoman made a quick, shy gesture towards

her, the strip of feather and velvet on her hair hovering like
a crimson hummingbird at the brim of her guest's gallantly
twisted felt.

Commercial offenses! And that easy, affectionate old fool
of a father of hers need never have broken the invaders'
law. It was not for motives of patriotism; just for money, of
which, anyway, they had enough. The Boches had requisi-
tioned the whole output of the Lille cotton mill for which he
was chief salesman, but a small trickle of goods managed to
get out to retailers by the back door. Her father met a supposed Dutch buyer. No sooner had the documents and the
cash changed hands than he found a pistol in the pit of his
stomach. The penalty was indefinite imprisonment, and
could be death.

Clémence, then seventeen, called at the office of the Gestapo. The major in command had the reputation — well, not
exactly of a woman hunter, but of oversentimentality. He
compensated for his brutal trade by a tenderness for youth,
especially if it were feminine. Clémence knew his character.
They all discussed and studied the weak points of their
individual oppressors with devotion as meticulous as that
of a university professor trying to recover meaning in a text
hopelessly corrupt.

"He did not exist," Clémence said.

"No," agreed the German, following her train of thought,
though the major had never been mentioned at all. "He was
the kind of man who can persuade himself every week that
he is in love."

Clémence was allowed to see him, perhaps because it
never occurred to her that she would not be. Even then she

had the Frenchwoman's medieval gift of arousing both chivalry and passion. The major emerged with an air of military courtesy from behind his desk and sat down beside her.

What she intended — but at seventeen it was hard to analyze what one intended. If the major were to kiss her, she would not resist, but what did one do then? And whatever one did, would it make any difference? She supposed that there ought to be a promise to release her father. Or would that be too much to ask at once? Prices and promises were never, surely, very direct. The thing to do was to excite his interest and soften it, not buy it, into pity.

The major was slimily correct. He pretended to be amused by her visit in a patronizing, almost paternal manner, but his eyes were uncomfortably admiring. It was going to be easy to make him believe that he attracted her. He sent for the file on her father.

This woman, now lunching with her, had brought it in and, for a little while, remained. In her presence Clémence behaved with the dignity proper to a *jeune fille* of good family. She was not sure whether the cause was just shame before an older woman, or whether it was the sudden example of a grace and maturity which, German or not, she envied. Instinct cried out to her that to exploit her seductive youth was not the right way, that to the secretary it would appear a betrayal of — of whatever affinity they had.

"What a bizarre thing is friendship!" Clémence murmured.

"But we had everything in common," the German answered decisively. "Everything which matters, that is."

"I could not count on that. It never occurred to me. You were just — of my world, when nothing else was."

Yet there had been no challenge or appeal whatever in the meeting of eyes. Both had been completely neutral. But when the secretary left the room Clémence treated the Gestapo major as if he had been a French civil servant — a police commissioner whom one expected to listen without interposing any personal relationship beyond a formal compliment. He responded with a detached politeness. The extenuating circumstances which Mademoiselle had been good enough to bring to his notice would be considered, but the law must regrettably take its course.

On her way out, accusing herself of cowardice, of an idiotic squeamishness, she passed through an anteroom where the secretary sat at her typewriter among shelves of files.

"When I left the major's office, how did you know?" Clémence asked. "Or did you know?"

"Of course I did! It was obvious that — how shall I put it? — that you had broken your sword over your knee. The face of a girl after a little triumph, even if she were disgusted with herself — wouldn't you recognize it?"

"You asked me if you could help."

"Did I? So openly?" The German smiled. "I suppose it was essential to be frank quickly."

"I loved the way you carried yourself, Herta."

"For me it was your voice."

The conversation had been, then as now, all composed of omissions. The secretary had complimented Clémence upon the beauty of her hair. Clémence offered to send her a packet of shampoo of prewar quality, forgetting that it was impossible legally to buy it. The German accepted gladly.

"But don't tell me where it comes from," she reminded the girl.

It was extraordinary that on so short an acquaintance the reminder should have been necessary.

"What am I to do?" Clémence had asked.

The secretary glanced contemptuously through her father's file.

"These penalties are so stupid!" she exclaimed. "At the most he deserves a fine of fifty thousand francs."

Clémence was again compelled to think in terms of the unfamiliar. She had heard, like everyone else, that some of the employees of the Gestapo were not above adding to their pay. She had decided nearly at once that this splendid older woman did not intend a hint.

The maître d'hôtel presented in its copper chafing dish the woodcock ordered for her guest. Clémence inspected it closely, and raised three fingers in approval.

"One is very doubtful at seventeen," she said. "All that one is going to be is already there, but one cannot know it."

"I was so angry with myself."

"We are thinking of the same thing, Herta?"

"Fifty thousand francs? One makes such remarks forgetting what they might mean. And when I saw you hesitate I could have killed myself. There was no time for explanations. Either we trusted each other or nothing mattered."

The woodcock flamed under the match. Clémence composedly withdrew her immense and charming sleeves. She heard her own strained voice at seventeen asking if a fine were impossible, and dreading the answer.

"Impossible. But, my dear, your father will be home tomorrow."

The secretary pinned the papers together and transferred them bodily to another file.

"Release and keep under surveillance," she explained. "There are so many of them who give orders. No one will ever question it."

"Oh, thank you! Thank you!"

"Try to keep him from being a fool. I could not do it twice."

"What shall I tell my father?"

"I should not tell him anything. He would only misunderstand."

"They find it so difficult to believe that women can be friends."

"My dear," said the secretary, opening the door for her, "they do not even know how to salute one another without using their hands."

Constant Lover

HAVE you ever insulted a man without speaking to him, without anything more than a casual meeting of eyes? I did, and the injustice of my thoughts about him still haunts me. I will give you the evidence just as it was presented to me. You may be cleverer than I was.

I was lunching alone in a Soho restaurant — a pleasant little place, expensive only if you wish it to be, without any uniformed porter outside the door or any chromium plate inside. It runs to lace curtains and red plush seats round the wall. At least they give the old-fashioned impression of red plush.

Across the room to my left a man and a girl were sitting at a corner table, close enough for me to watch them, not so close that I could hear what they were saying. There appeared to be some eighteen or twenty years between their ages. The fellow looked as if he spent a couple of hours at his barber twice a week, perfecting the lie of his gray hair and smoothing the wrinkles out of his distinguished skin. He might have been a quack doctor pretending to be a fashionable surgeon, or an unsuccessful actor modeling himself upon a matinee idol of thirty years ago, or a movie producer trying to resemble the illustration of a diplomat in a woman's magazine. All that was certain was pretense.

His manner was intolerably affected. It did not fit his maturity or his quiet and luxurious clothes. He kept fidgeting with his glasses, putting them on to read the menu, taking them off to show he did not need them, putting them on again to regard waiters and customers with a faintly defiant patronage. He was determined to impress us all, and especially his companion, that there could be nothing wrong with a world in which he talked and existed.

The girl with him seemed as resentful as I of his affectations. She showed no interest in the delicately feminine meal which he had ordered for her. She made no reply, or the shortest, to his remarks. His conversation, continually restarted, was so forcedly gallant in approach and so emptily bright in delivery that perhaps no reply was demanded.

She was disillusioned to a point of utter demoralization. She had not even bothered to put powder and lipstick on her pale, heavy face. I could see it was not used to such deprivation. In the evening, with a little patience, it must have recovered some most attractive remains of youth. She stared in front of her, giving me the impression that she would as soon be dead as play the game of conversation any longer. She might have been trying to cut him, his presence and his memory right out of her life. He was something she had once treasured and simply could not bear any more.

I ruled out at once all the normal relationships between two generations. Even if he were godfather or family solicitor and the lunch a boring duty, there would be an occasional smile, some sort of flirtation with the harmless old friend, however tiresome. Conjecture worried away at the problem. When alone and expansive, one insists on entertaining oneself with fantasies, but they must be logical enough to entertain a companion if he or she were there.

His wife or divorced wife, then? No, there was not even a resentful intimacy. So I fitted her into my possible world as a young woman who had been too fascinated by all that profile and perfection and had discovered, after a week or a month of both of them, that there was little else. I wondered if he kept putting on and taking off his glasses when he wore pajamas.

Much as I loathed that artificial middle-aged man, I could not help feeling — when my bottle was empty and my speculations more charitable — that she was taking too seriously her weariness of him, whatever the reasons for it. After all, the fellow had his qualities. He was behaving for his public as if there were nothing wrong whatever; and that was bitterly hard to do by the side of a person whose only contribution had been a short speech of exasperation, unless the pattern into which she was rolling innumerable bread pills had some significance.

He offered her a liqueur. She refused it. He took a brandy himself and lit a cigar. He looked at me. On my side of the room the restaurant had thinned, and I had become his only audience. *There's nothing wrong,* his eyes said to me, *nothing which can't be put right in time.* He was determined to ignore the irrevocable disaster. By ignoring it, it ceased to exist. A typical reaction of the desperate male.

He paid his bill and fussed gallantly over her gloves and bag. While he was taking his hat from the attendant, she, too, seemed to accept me as a public. She shrugged her shoulders at me — or made some other disloyal little gesture — as much as to ask how the devil a girl was supposed to stand things forever.

I left the restaurant. An hour later those two had faded from all but an occasional memory. My imaginative world had died for its creator, and it had no right to live again, to collide with our common world, to muddle itself with justice.

I have never since set eyes on that immaculate pretender, but his pale young woman I met again. She was no longer emotionally dead — at any rate in outward appearance — and her make-up was now vivid and in need of repair. The swing door of a pub just off the Charing Cross Road catapulted her at me. The place was only a hundred yards from the restaurant where I had first seen her. That fringe of theater land may have been her world, though she had probably no professional status, theatrical or other. To judge by her accent and what was left of her bearing, I should say that she had a small income of her own, and that she belonged by right to Knightsbridge but found drinking in Soho more to her taste.

She clung to me for physical support and addressed me as Ronnie. Then, talking fast and heartily to herself as much as to me, she said that of course I wasn't Ron: I was the man who had stared at her when she was having lunch with her father.

Father and daughter. That was a relationship I had dismissed at once. The age difference did not seem enough, and the manner was all wrong. A woman can show contempt for her father or anger, but not that bored, hopeless indifference with which she treats a stupid and unwanted lover.

I repeated vaguely the word *father*, recalling the man of pretenses, so nervously eager to persuade the restaurant and her that they were two people of distinction who had every right to draw attention to themselves.

"He is on the stage?" I asked.

"Stage? Hell, no! Government contractor, all dressed up to impress the beak! He had just bailed me out that morning. He'll never let anyone see he's ashamed of me, Ron. I'll say that for the old fool."

Eggs As Ain't

MRS. Swallop had been working her twenty-acre holding singlehanded ever since Tom Swallop was killed in the Boer War when she was seventeen years old and a six months' bride. He left her his scrap of freehold land, no child, and apparently so pleasant a memory that she preferred to live with it rather than change her status.

Her farm — if you can call it a farm — was up at the end of a grass track: a patch of cultivation in a dry bottom surrounded by the thorn and bracken on the slopes, and well fenced except for short stretches of queer material such as old bed springs and rusty sheets of corrugated iron. It had a name on the map, but no one for ten miles round ever called it anything but Noah's Ark.

The birds and animals were not, however, in Biblical couples. Mrs. Swallop stocked her land with breeding females, for she had her own ways of encouraging them. There were two enormous turkey hens, a goose, a saddle-backed sow, a flock of undisciplined chickens, a black cow, a black nanny goat and a big black cat who was fierce as a watchdog when she had kittens. The only representative of the male sex was a buck rabbit who attended to the comfort of several prolific does.

She was a bright and cleanly old body — so far as one can be when farming alone — but her dress and her ways were odd. She might be wearing an old tweed skirt below an upper half swathed in sacking, or a new purple jersey with a horse blanket for a skirt. She had a black mustache, and she used to whisper under it to her animals.

Mrs. Swallop would whisper for her neighbors, too, if she liked them; so they were always ready to lend her a male when she turned up, driving one of her females in front of her or pushing it, squawking, in the large dilapidated perambulator which was her only farm transport. If there was anything else in the bottom of the pram, such as eggs or cream, they would buy it from her by some careful method which would not draw the attention of Percy Crott.

Those were the days just after the war when farmers were making a lot more money than now. On the other hand, they had to put up with fellows like Crott. He had been a village schoolmaster till one of his fourteen-year-olds sent him to hospital; and when he came out he got a job in the Ministry of Food. How he rose to be an inspector, no one ever discovered — for all he knew about food was the regulations to prevent the public from eating it. He had a blotchy pink face as smooth as a pig's, with a nasty little mouth in the middle of it and a round chin which he used to stick out when he was speaking — like one of those businessmen who are so proud of their faces that they put their pictures in the advertisements in spite of the sales they must lose.

Crott could never catch the big farmers, who generally obeyed the law, and had a dozen inspector-proof ways of covering themselves up when they didn't. If he wanted to bring a neighbor before the courts and make an example of him, he went for the little man, who was sure to be breaking regulations because he had no time to read them. And he made a dead set at Mrs. Swallop because she built a breeding hutch for the rabbits out of all the pamphlets and government forms which the postman brought her. Those rabbits fairly flourished under the welfare state, but when Percy Crott saw the hutch he said it was a scandal, and carried on as if Mrs. Swallop had built it out of a stack of Bibles.

All the same, it was difficult to find an offense by which he could put her out of business. She had no books or accounts — for she insisted that she could not write — and old Trancard was always ready to tell any lie for her. Crott's only hope was to catch her red-handed selling eggs to the public.

Trancard took a very friendly interest in the old lady, for his sheep run surrounded her land on the north and east, and the luck he had with the lambing was marvelous. He guessed what Percy Crott was up to when he saw him hiding behind a hedge and counting Mrs. Swallop's birds. So he persuaded her to turn over a new leaf and register herself as a poultry producer.

"It won't give 'ee no trouble at all, missus," he told her. "I'm a licensed packer, and you hand over your eggs to me for grading and packing, and get paid by the government at fifty shillings for ten dozen. But what you must not do, missus, is to sell 'em to anyone who ain't licensed. And if that young Crott catches you at it, you'll fetch up before the beaks."

"I don't want no more of 'is papers," Mrs. Swallop answered.

"Ain't no papers, not to speak of, me dear! You delivers your eggs to me whenever you happens to be passing, and along comes the money and your National Poultry Food regular. If you mixes it up with a bit of barley, which maybe I can find for 'ee, the hens won't hardly know what they're eatin'. Oh, it's all as easy as kiss your 'and, missus, begging your pardon," he said.

Trancard was obviously making money out of his fine flock of Rhode Island Reds, so Mrs. Swallop decided to take his advice. While there was plenty she wouldn't understand, there was nothing she couldn't, once she got her lips moving silently round the problem. She collected another score of hens, one by one wherever a bird caught her eye, and a shocking lot of mixed breeds they were; but she soon had them in the pink of condition and laying up and down the hedgerows as fast as if they had been their orderly sisters in Trancard's deep litter house.

When Mrs. Swallop came up with her third load of eggs, six inches deep in the bottom of the pram, Trancard graded them and gave two dozen back to her. They were too small or too crooked.

"And what must I do wi' 'em, mister?" she asked.

"Do what you likes with 'em. The government don't want 'em."

"They be all egg inside," she said.

"But the public won't buy 'em in the shops, missus."

"Can I sell 'em," she asked, "without that young Crott comin' up after me wi' the constable?"

"No, you can't. Not, to say, sellin' 'em as *is* sellin' 'em. But you can give 'em away, and I'll tell 'ee where. And that's Mr. Buckfast up at The Bull, with all his guests wanting two fried eggs to their breakfasts when he can't hardly give 'em one. He'll take all you give 'im, and it wouldn't surprise me if 'e was to pay you at seventy bob instead of the fifty we gets from the government. But 'e won't be paying you for eggs, mind, but for carrots or suchlike."

Mrs. Swallop leaned against the gatepost, calculating in so fast a whisper that she couldn't keep listening to herself; so she fell into a sort of trance, and old Trancard had to take her up to the house and bring her round with a glass of port.

"And there's no point in you bringing eggs as ain't legal eggs up to me for grading," he said, when he had given her an arm back to the pram. "You know an egg as ain't when you sees it as well as I do. But don't you go giving away an egg that's an egg within the meaning of the order, because it's not worth the risk."

Next week it was all over the district that Mrs. Swallop had another male to keep the buck rabbit company. He was a black Leghorn cock of a fine laying strain, with a certificate to prove it; but his breastbone was twisted over to one side like a plowshare, so that when he stretched out his neck to crow he had to spread his tail the other way to balance himself. Mrs. Swallop, naturally enough, did not have to pay a penny for him, though she may have done some little favor to the bees in passing.

In spite of his looks the hens took to this young cripple, as females will. And Mrs. Swallop groomed his tail feathers and whispered to him and stuffed him with National Poultry

Food till the old buck was so jealous that he set about him and got a spur down his earhole before they could be separated.

When spring came, Mrs. Swallop was not delivering anything like the proper number of eggs, in spite of the fact that she and the black Leghorn between them had raised her flock to nearly a hundred birds, most of them laying pullets of her own breeding. Trancard went down to her holding to see if he could help at all, and a repulsive sight the yard was for a careful farmer. He stared at those miscolored, lopsided, sinister-looking freak pullets, and went purple in the face with the pressure of all he did not like to say.

"Why, what's wrong wi' 'em?" she asked him.

"Missus," he said, "there's everything wrong with 'em. But if they're yourn, they're laying — and that young Crott has been up, lookin' at me books."

Mrs. Swallop gave him a sly smile under her mustache, with a twitch of the lips that must have enchanted Tom Swallop fifty years before.

"Don't 'ee worry over me, me dear," she said.

But Trancard did worry. He knew Mrs. Swallop was making a mysterious profit. So did Percy Crott. She had had her fences repaired, and a pipe laid to the spring where she got her water instead of old lengths of rusty gutter stopped with clay. And there was nothing to account for all the eggs in town, especially at The Bull, except the visits of Mrs. Swallop's pram.

Crott timed it nicely. He watched Mrs. Swallop deliver a parcel of eggs — which should have been all she produced

— to Trancard, and he let her go on down to the town with her pram. Then he took his government car and the local cop from behind the haystack where he had parked the pair of them, and drove into Trancard's yard and asked to see the books.

Old Trancard tried to muddle him by passing off some of his own eggs as Mrs. Swallop's. The cop did his best to help. But the ink was hardly dry in the book, and there was no getting away from the figures. Mrs. Swallop had delivered only two dozen eggs that morning, and nothing else for a week.

"She'll be on her way to The Bull now, constable," said Percy Crott, pushing him into the car.

He started to drive slowly down the hill so as to reach the hotel about the same time as Mrs. Swallop. All Trancard could do was to rumble along behind in a tractor, wondering how Mrs. Swallop could ever pay the fifty pounds or so which the beaks would have to fine her, and whether they would give her six months if she didn't.

When they stopped in front of The Bull, Percy Crott and the constable nipped round into the back yard, with Trancard a second or two behind them trying to look as if he had just called to return the empties. There was Mrs. Swallop talking to Buckfast, the proprietor.

"Madam," asked the inspector, "what have you got in that perambulator?"

"Nothing but eggs, sir. Nothing at all," she answered, pretending she was frightened of the cop.

"And were you thinking of selling them?"

"No, she weren't," Buckfast told him pretty sharply. "She was giving them to me. And it's legal."

"Uncommonly kind of her!" said Percy Crott in a sarcastic way, and he whipped the cover off the pram.

It was stuffed with eggs. And not one of them was fairly oval. There were eggs which might have been fat white sausages, and round eggs and oblongs and lozenges, and pear-shaped eggs and eggs with a twist like a gibbous moon with round points.

Inspector Crott pushed them aside with the tips of his fingers as if they were something the dog had been rolling in. They were all the same quality right down to the bottom of the pram.

"Don't your hens lay anything fit for human consumption?" he asked.

"No, sir," she told him, "they don't. A poor old woman can't afford good 'ens like you gentlemen."

Then Buckfast was taken with a fit of the sniggers, and old Trancard slapped his breeches and grinned at Mrs. Swallop as if she were the knowingest farmer in all the county.

"Damme if she ain't been breeding for rejects!" he roared. "Damme, and I tried to tell 'er how to run fowls! I tell you, Mr. Percy Crott, that if only she 'ad a cock with a face like yourn, them 'ens would lay eggs and bacon, and burst out laughin' when they turned their 'eads round to look at what they 'ad done," he said.

Letter to a Sister

DEAREST CONCHITA,

You will have had my telegram that I am in Lima. I could not have stayed another day on that ship. I *had* to leave it.

Do not let Mama be worried. As we all told her, it is perfectly correct in these days for an unmarried woman to travel alone. No one showed me the slightest disrespect.

I am quite well, and I am not in love — at least not in the usual sense. I am remaining here for a few days before I continue my journey up the coast to join Papa in Panama. I have of course sent a telegram to him, too. What has happened is nearly unbelievable.

You remember the untidy foreigner who came on board, singing, at Valparaíso when you were saying good-by to me, and saluted us all with such exaggerated politeness that we thought he must be drunk. He and I turned out to be the only passengers. He was traveling on the *Naarden* only as far as Peru, so I had no reason to discourage him. Besides, there was no one else to talk to.

The German captain and his officers were appallingly formal. I would not like to marry a German; it would be difficult to call him by his Christian name. And the officers would stare at my face, which I hate. I can always tell what people are like by the way they look at me. Those who are

truly kind forget all about my disfigurement after the first
few minutes. I do not mean that they try to forget. They
really do. Are you surprised at my mentioning what we
never speak of?

The tall foreigner was an Englishman, and of tradition!
Our grandfathers always said they were mad, but people of
our generation have found them most dull and respectable.
Now I know what our grandfathers meant.

His name was unpronounceable. It was written Har-
borough-Jones. He said that he was once a major in the
Horse Guards of the Queen of England, but that he found it
ridiculous to use the title of rank while traveling in jams and
jellies.

Jams and jellies! You would expect them to be sold by a
fat Greek from Argentina, not a major in an aristocratic regiment! I could not tell what he really was, and it would have
been useless to press him for an answer. He amused himself
by making the wildest fantasies sound like truth. Even when
sober, his imagination was out of control.

He spoke Spanish with a queer, clipped accent and tremendous gusto. I think our language and our Latin-Ameri-
can civilization intoxicated him as much as the glass which
was too frequently in his hand. He told me that when he
spoke English he was quite a different person and of the
utmost propriety.

"I have no sympathy for Major Francis Harborough-
Jones," he said. "The man I like is Don Francisco Jones y
Harborough."

You will see that he had the mixture of nobility and crazi-
ness which we all adore. He behaved to me at once as if I

were a daughter from whom he had long been absent. Mama will think that an impertinence. But I liked it. I am so shy with strangers. With him I could be gay as I only dare to be at home. He made me feel completely irresponsible, as if nothing in life mattered but to enjoy it. I forgot my loneliness and that doctors could not help me without leaving a scar as hideous as what they removed. If he had been twenty years younger I should have fallen desperately in love.

On the last evening before the ship reached Lima, where Don Francisco was to disembark, we were sitting together as usual on deck. I will give you his own words as exactly as I can remember them, and you must fancy that you are listening to a play. My own deep voice you can imagine; his was always loud and kind and laughing. Think of Papa telling us stories in bed, and how there was nothing we could believe but his affection.

"I should like to give a party tomorrow in the ship's lounge," he said, "if I can get the permission of the other passenger and the purser."

I replied that of course he had my permission, and asked if the party was for his customers.

"Buy, buy my jams and jellies!" he called like a street vendor. "Very cheap, my jams and jellies!"

"But calm, Don Francisco!" I begged him.

"Yes, my daughter. I shall not leave out the customers. But I want the President of the Republic if he will come. The generals and the admirals and all the Children of the Sun! What joy, what joy is Spanish America!"

"Would it not be better to give the party on shore?"

"Dearest" — he used such words most improperly, but as he was a foreigner I forgave him — "dearest, it would indeed! But the fact is that in Peru I cannot give a party because I am not allowed to pay for anything."

That must, I thought, be due to some misunderstanding. The Peruvians are no more hospitable than the rest of us. We all entertain a foreign visitor as well and as long as we can; but eventually — at any rate in commercial circles — he is allowed to pay.

I asked him if he would let me suggest some delicate way of returning hospitality. He insisted that it was utterly impossible. And off he went again upon his love for our Americas, as eloquently as any politician upon Independence Day. The long glass at his side was frequently refilled by the steward, who had orders to watch it and take it away when it was empty. He called that being refueled in the air.

I refused to have my curiosity deflected.

"But why, Don Francisco," I persisted, "are you not allowed to pay for anything in Peru?"

"Because, little one," he answered superbly, "I am descended from the conqueror Pizarro and the daughter of the Inca Atahualppa."

"So at last I know why you wear a bath towel instead of trousers," I replied, pretending to believe him and throwing back the ball.

Such was his usual dress in the morning — a bath towel and an old tweed coat. The first time he appeared in my presence like that I intended to show myself a little cold, but a moment later I was giggling childishly at the look the captain gave him.

We went to dinner — he at the officers' table and I, by preference, alone. When I had finished, I waited on deck for him. It was his habit to sit on for half an hour over his wine, amusing himself if none of the officers remained to amuse him. That was, he said, an English ceremony.

As it was our last evening and still he did not come, I went down to my cabin for a book, but he was not in the saloon. On my return, as I passed the ship's office, I saw the purser standing in the doorway and pounding his fist into his hand with one of those clumsy gestures of Northerners who do not know by nature how to gesticulate. Don Francisco, who was opposite him in the passage, must have been much angrier than he appeared; but he only smiled down at the purser and swayed a little at the knees.

The purser was shouting in English. He was a man without manners, as I think the Nazis must have been — nothing but a white uniform buttoned too tightly over bad temper. He had twice been rude to me. You will not believe it, but he made me declare that my disfigurement was not infectious. He resented the presence of a single woman among males.

There is no dignity in the English language when men are excited. The purser was swallowing hard, and croaking:

"Jam, jam, ja-a-am! Jam, jam, ja-a-am! Here you will not sell your ja-a-am! No and no! I forbid you to give your party. The *Naarden* is a German ship, not a grocery shop!"

Naturally I passed them as quickly as I could, and did not watch until I was sure they could not see me. Don Francisco was being very mischievous. Evidently he had given up all hope of obtaining his request. He had no interest at all in calming the purser. He smiled and weaved his tall body over him like a snake above a fat frog. He patted him on the shoulder and warned him that he should be careful, that after a heavy dinner in the tropics a man of his build might easily have a stroke. And when the purser began to insult the English in general, he waved him back into the office with the gesture of one who shoos away a fly.

I was sitting in the darkness of the boat deck when Don Francisco joined me. After we had talked a little while, he said to me that curiosity killed the cat. The proverbs of his people are coarser than our own.

I answered with dignity that if it had been I who wished to talk to the purser, I should not have approached him at that hour. Everyone knew that he liked to shut himself up in his office after his oversolid evening meal. He even had a notice of VERBOTEN on his door.

Don Francisco admitted humbly that I was perfectly right, and that indeed the purser, unlike the majority of men, was less approachable after dinner than before. For that reason he himself had been particularly tactful, he said, and had knocked his forehead three times upon the purser's counter and kissed the ground.

And then, at last permitting himself some slight loss of self-control, he began to curse the purser for an unbelieving, unimaginative Kraut — which means, I think, a cabbage. And after swearing like a gaucho, though most delicately changing the words, he translated some English oaths. At any rate they were quite unlike our own and far less reasonable. It is permissible to guess at the parentage of someone who has insulted you, but you cannot anticipate the fate of his soul.

"And what astonishes me," he declared, "is that I damn the man so thoroughly and he is none the worse."

"Thank God for his mercies!" I answered.

He lay back in his chair and laughed.

"Well, it is true one would have to be careful. To phrase a curse which is meant so that it can be distinguished from a curse which is not — I do not know how my ancestors managed it."

"Pizarro? Or his Inca princess?" I asked — for you know how I adore the ridiculous, and I wanted him to recover his temper and entertain me.

"Neither," he replied. "From them I am descended on my mother's side. On my father's side we were always witches. Life is like that. To the rich comes more money. Upon the improbable it pours improbabilities. In my club there is a man who has the hereditary right to undress the bishop of his diocese and wash him in the River Thames. In winter he trains elephants. Why not? To him it is all perfectly natural."

One's breath is taken away by such flights of fancy. All I could find to say was that the bishop must be glad his friend had another occupation in winter.

Don Francisco answered that the bishop could be washed on demand, whatever the weather, and that I must not put any faith in the common illusion that the English were influenced by common sense. They always preferred the fantastic to the practical.

"My daughter," he said, "in England everything that has ever existed still exists. That is the kind of people we are. There was once a chief witch in Hereford. Therefore there is still a chief witch in Hereford. And I, who have the honor to be at your feet, am he."

"So it is due to your charms that we buy the Hereford cattle?"

"Not forgetting the jams and jellies."

"And we part tomorrow and you have never shown me yourself flying upon a broomstick."

"For that," he said, "one needs a familiar spirit — if it has ever been done, which I doubt."

"Dear Don Francisco, is there any spirit which is unfamiliar to you?"

He kissed my hand. It always delighted him when I enjoyed this sort of tennis with words, though I myself would wonder afterwards if I had not been too bitter.

"Have you never heard that the soul must be fed as well as the body?" he asked. "And, believe me, the sustenance it prefers is alcohol in moderation. Far better that than to take oneself too seriously and always be whispering *Down, Fido!* to something which would be happier in hell!"

"And without Fido?" I laughed. "Nothing to show me? Nothing at all?"

"I am not in practice," he replied. "I am a traditional figurehead — a mere administrator. Old women's tricks are all I know. Like the curing — perhaps — of warts."

Little sister, I did not answer anything. I do not think I even looked at him.

"That is all it is, you know," he said. "A giant wart which lives on you because it has no other home. I could take it away, if you believed."

I recovered myself at once, and told him that it was not a subject which my most intimate friends were permitted to discuss with me.

He was quite unconcerned by my rebuke. He stood over me, grinning as if he had just thought of still greater riches of impertinence.

"All the same, I want it," he said. "Do you give it to me?"

I answered passionately that I gave it to him with my whole heart. I do not quite know what I meant. But I was so sincere I could have struck him.

I am ashamed to tell you what happened. I can only say that I was fascinated by him and quite helpless; and the indignity was so swift. He spat on his finger and touched my disfigurement. Then he spat to the four points of the compass and did something with his hands in the darkness which I could not distinguish.

"And now, my daughter, it is good-by," he said. "You are outraged by me, and would not speak to me in the morning even if we had time to talk. I shall leave the ship early with the customs launch, and as the purser will not let me give my party I shall not return."

I could not trust myself to speak. I stared at him as one stares at a lover who has forgotten decency.

"Remember it is not what friends say at parting which matters," he told me, "but what they think about each other afterwards. Half I have done for you; the other half depends on your belief."

Conchita, I awoke in the morning utterly disgusted with myself. There might be some excuse for him, but *I* had not been drinking. What I had spoken of, and what I had allowed — all humiliated me.

I looked out of the porthole of my cabin. Two miles away were the low houses and docks and sands of Callao, the port of Lima. The customs launch was just leaving the *Naarden,* and Don Francisco was in it as he said he would be. It was the first time I had ever seen him well dressed. Immaculate, with a flower in his buttonhole.

When I came on deck, the ship was alongside the quay. I was most courteously saluted by a captain of police who addressed me by my name. He astonished me by saying that in case I wished to land and visit Lima a room in the best hotel had been reserved for me. He also presented to me the compliments of Don Francisco Jones y Harborough, who regretted that he was unavoidably prevented from escorting me since he had been commanded to accompany the Vice-President of the Republic on a visit to Cuzco.

Was I never to escape from his lunacy? I thanked the captain and remarked, controlling my voice as best I could, that it was not my custom to interrupt my travels at the request of foreigners.

"But Don Francisco does not count as a foreigner!" he exclaimed. "He is a descendant of Francisco Pizarro and Atahuallpa's daughter. There are only two of them left, and the other is old and in Spain and will die childless."

Who could have guessed that he was telling the truth? I went back to my cabin, with all my emotions shattered. The mirror faced me. As you know, I have trained myself not to notice a mirror any more than you, Conchita, the pavement under your feet. But the man's bad taste had made me conscious of that loathsome mark. And then, hating him and in tears, I suddenly realized that never would he have forgotten his courtesy and tenderness unless he believed in himself. What I believed I could not be sure.

That night, little sister, while the ship remained in harbor, I slept sweetly. I went to breakfast early. But no, I did not go to breakfast at all! I went no further than the door of the saloon. The purser was eating alone, and fingering a black mark on his cheek. I rushed back to my cabin, telling myself that I was a romantic fool. But the lower fragment of my growth had gone, and the skin was red like that of a healthy scar.

I packed, and I fled to the room in Lima which Don Francisco had so thoughtfully reserved for me. I remembered his words: that it lived on me because it had no other home. I could not go on to Panama. How could I ever have met the purser's eyes during a whole week — the week that has just passed — while hour by hour I was returning so eagerly to my mirror?

The Brides of Solomon

IN SPITE of heat, insects and isolation, Don Felipe had made himself comfortable. He had two more years to serve in the Peruvian forest, administrating the headwaters of the Madre de Dios, and every reason to believe that he would finish them with some remnants of health and a reputation as a reasonable man. He preferred his cool office to the jungle. That, too, was reasonable. It was the first duty of a government servant to be easily and courteously accessible.

He was intimidated — though he did not for a moment show it — by the determined Diocesan Visitor who had so smoothly come up from the river. Father Hilario held himself most unnecessarily upright in the curves of his basket chair. He seemed to set an awkward standard not only for administrators of Indian territory but for the flowers and creepers which rioted over the patio and were so obviously and carelessly growing when compared with the rigid black figure of the Diocesan Visitor.

"It is true, then, that this Englishman has two hundred wives?" Father Hilario asked.

"If one believed all one heard," answered Don Felipe with a prudent wave of the hand by which he hoped to dismiss the subject, "there would be no end to investigations."

"You have not confirmed the rumor yourself?"

"I cannot afford to be absent from my post so long, Padre. And for what? There is no objection to a serious anthropologist living among the Indians."

"Provided he confines himself to the interests of science," Father Hilario said. "But this Englishman is conducting a mission."

"I do not remember that he had any interest at all in religion."

"It is nine years since you saw him."

Don Felipe looked surprised. Time ran away while one occupied oneself at leisurely government pace. But it was indeed all of nine years since Solomon Carver had called on him with — after a full measure of formal courtesies — the bald statement that he intended to go into the forest and study a primitive tribe. Don Felipe told him that he would not be allowed to do any such thing, that the days were long past when you could paddle up the rivers and establish, if you lived, a mission or a private army or your own little slave state. Peruvian policy was all against irresponsible interference with the Indians.

"Here as elsewhere," Don Felipe had explained to Carver, "he who desires to serve must be appointed to do so."

"I am."

"But by whom?"

"Myself," Carver said.

Don Felipe pointed out that he had been thinking of some official body like a botanical or geographical society.

"If you mean," replied Carver, "that I must be vouched for by any committee which will take the trouble to print a few letterheads and obtain some half-witted minor royalty for a patron, then I will see that it is done."

Being a son of parents so poor that his career could only be made in territory where no one else would serve, Don Felipe was bewildered by the arrogance of an ancient university. He perceived, however, that his decayed bungalow, commanding nothing but a landing stage, a handful of demoralized military and a collection of thatched roofs hardly distinguishable from the surrounding forest, was being invited into partnership against the whole easily impressionable world.

"It will take me a month," said Solomon Carver.

It took him two. When the plane from Lima set him down once more on the river, his credentials were in perfect order and described him as an anthropologist.

The Diocesan Visitor, disapprovingly silent while Don Felipe repeated this conversation, replied at once that Carver indeed had influential friends. The suave inquiries of the Church had found out everything about the man. Before the war, a lecturer on anthropology and comparative religion. A serious and too self-sufficient colonel at the end of the war. And then, in his early forties, he had considered it his duty to reject civilization, earnestly proclaiming that there was no other hope for the future of humanity but intensified study of its beginnings. That in itself, Father Hilario insisted, was a doctrine which might lead to all kinds of aberration.

Don Felipe did not agree, but had no wish to argue with authority. From the government point of view it was far more important that he should be able to reply to consuls and relatives that Carver was safe and well, and that no unseemly expedition was required to look for him.

News of the man had filtered down from Indian to Indian, and Indian to trader, and trader to Don Felipe's office. He had wandered about among the tribes who understood a little Spanish, learning their languages and how to keep alive. He had penetrated further and further into the vaporous gorges where the Amazon forests became the Andes, and settled down at last with the dying, melancholy Icuari. Apparently he had found what he wanted, or they had.

His polygamy was a fact. Down the years the number of wives credited to Carver had grown from forty to two hundred. Don Felipe had once or twice considered whether it might not be his business to remonstrate with him; but it was never urgent business. The Icuari were not — by the standards of the Amazon — particularly difficult to reach; they were just of no interest. They had neither mines nor trade nor cultivated clearings nor a navigable river. Water cataracted into their country or shot out of high caves like jets from giant hose pipes.

"He has gone native," said Don Felipe. "That is regrettable, but of no importance."

Father Hilario stabbed with two restless fingers at the report which lay on the administrator's desk, as if laying anathema upon it. It was the report which had brought him up the river. It came from Bolivia; it was detailed and official; and it stated that Carver was not an anthropologist at all but some sort of Protestant missionary in disguise.

"And that is of very great importance," he pronounced. "When Anglo-Saxons give themselves to their peculiar religions, they become enraged as mad dogs."

"You have no idea of what it means, Father," Don Felipe protested in a voice of official caution. "Twelve days by launch, eight by canoe, weeks when we shall be wading rather than walking, and without food for the porters."

"When did you last undertake the regulation tour of your district?"

"*Bueno! Bueno!* But when I am away, there is no one to attend to the correspondence."

"Your secretary, perhaps . . ."

Don Felipe made a last, hopeless attempt to avert the inevitable.

"Look, Father — is it likely, this story of wives? Doubtless it arises only from the unfortunate name with which his godparents presented him. Down here it is hard enough for a man of taste to find one tolerable woman, let alone two hundred."

The Diocesan Visitor showed the teeth of the Church as well as his own in a formal smile.

"But if the doctrines of this man of taste — whatever they may be — were to spread to Christian Indians, you realize that my bishop would be bound to protest to Lima."

Don Felipe surrendered. He gave orders that his camp equipment be packed and that the white-and-gold uniform by which he was accustomed to impress the more accessible native chiefs be left behind. He knew as much about travel in the forest as any trader's headman; that was why he had used all possible tact to avoid it.

The river journey turned out to be more tolerable than he expected. In thirteen days — four by launch and nine by canoe — the party reached the end of the navigable waterways and the last of the Indians who had any regular dealings with the white man. Father Hilario, having got his way, was an excellent companion. He was quick to adjust his approach to any objective. Severity towards officialdom. Considerate and amusing manners in camp.

He also had patience — and that, as soon as they set foot on comparatively dry land, was an indispensable quality. Carver and his Icuari could only be reached by choosing the right valley to follow. The ridges ran more or less parallel to the Cordillera, and each was a range of mountains in its own right. Sheer cliff and impassable forest barred all crossing from one valley to the next.

Neither map nor instinct was the least help. A guide who knew the gorges was essential. The first deliberately wasted time. Don Felipe, who was mild as the Indians themselves, dismissed him with courtesy after four desperate days in the bed of a torrent. The second insisted that they had taken the wrong tributary of the Madre de Dios, and that they must return down-river and try again. Don Felipe stood by his own notes. True, he had compiled them in his flowery patio, but the facts of geography were more easily seen from a basket chair than the bottom of a gorge; he knew that his route was not so mistaken as all that.

The third guide, obtained when food was already beginning to run short, had traded with the Icuari and had no doubt whatever of the path. He insisted that a white man had persuaded the tribe to leave the dripping forest and take to high ground. Their country could be reached in three days' march.

Don Felipe understood that confidence had been established and that this at last was the truth. He decided to send his men downstream to the launch and to food, and to go on alone with Father Hilario.

"Ask him about the two hundred wives," ordered the Visitor, who did not speak the language of the river sources.

The Indian, not being sure of any numbers over ten, replied to Don Felipe's question:

"The cacique has as many as there are stars, and all dressed in white."

Feeling a natural sympathy for anyone who merely desired to be left in peace, Don Felipe was reluctant to stir up trouble before he had to. He translated tactfully:

"He says that when we get nearer to the stars, we shall see women dressed in white."

"You see!" exclaimed Father Hilario. "The fellow is teaching some sort of Mohammedan paradise!"

"Very likely."

"And false doctrines travel as far and as fast as the true. This Salomón must leave the country at once."

In the next two days they approached the stars a deal nearer than suited either Don Felipe, who believed in letting a mule do his climbing, or Father Hilario, who usually carried his bishop's authority by canoe. The guide's route, hardly ever perceptible as a path, would have nothing to do with water and rose seven thousand feet to the top of a ridge.

Forty miles to the west, across canyon after canyon unexplorable by anything but vegetation, they could see the mists recoiling from the sheer cliffs and graveled slopes of the Cordillera Oriental. Don Felipe looked longingly at the edge of the high Peru which was his true homeland. To reach that glimpse of bare skyline would mean, he reckoned, a journey of over six weeks, down the rivers to the frontier of Brazil and Bolivia and then up again.

"And now?" he asked the guide, dreading lest the appalling gorge beneath them should have to be crossed, and the ridge beyond it climbed.

"Not far. We sleep here."

Slow questioning revealed that they were within three hours of the nearest Icuari village; but the guide was unwilling to appear at dusk without warning — though he agreed that the tribe was very peaceful and had no firearms, not even the white man. He spoke of them, now that he was on the edge of their country, with almost religious respect.

Don Felipe was surprised at his tone. The Icuari, so far as he knew, were still in a state of transition from food gathering to agriculture — hardly better, in fact, than a dejected band of apes which had retreated westward from war and the rivers to die, alone, in the uninhabitable country of the spray.

The two Peruvians and their guide slept in the shelter of an overhanging cliff where campfires had been numerous enough to burn the moss from the rock. In the morning their path entered a cleared and beaten track. The ridge broadened and then dipped to a saddle. Looking down on it, they could see huts and cultivated clearings among the trees. A white-robed woman crossed from shadow to shadow.

"It is true!" exclaimed Father Hilario, eager with indignation.

Don Felipe, who had expected nothing more than the hardly visible, timid shelters of savages, was far more impressed by the signs of a purposeful community than by the flicker of white. There was even an alignment of huts; you could almost call it a street. He guardedly expressed his surprise, and was conscious of a humble pleasure that there below them was a situation which could not be bullied into shape by any Diocesan Visitor.

Having no other evidence of his rank and importance, he assumed an official bearing and preceded Father Hilario into the village. There was a reserved welcome. It was clear that the Icuari expected them and had no fear. The men were the usual bobbed-haired, stocky, copper creatures of the forest, but they carried no arms and their manners were self-assured rather than chattering.

Most of the women were heavy, apathetic and busy with objectless activities; but among them moved a kind of Wellsian elite, all very young and dressed in sacklike tunics of white cotton confined at the waist by brilliantly dyed cords. They looked competent — the last quality one would expect, Father Hilario thought, in idle and corrupted women. Yet there could be no doubt who they were. The devil, too, could sing a psalm when he wished. And why were all the visible children — plenty of them — between the ages of two and four?

Out of the trees, upon the edge of which the children were playing, came a European woman, severely dressed and freshly laundered. She greeted the party in blunt but fairly efficient Spanish, and invited them to accompany her to the upper village.

Invited? It was an order from the matron. Don Felipe explained that he and his companion were by no means the casual and predatory travelers they looked, but the administrator of the district and the representative of the bishop.

"We know that already, Don Felipe," she answered, "and we are all very glad you have come."

"How did you get here, Sister?" he asked, knowing that she had never passed through his territory.

"From Bolivia."

"On foot?"

"On foot. It takes weeks, but it is not really difficult since Señor Carver made the track. A wonderful man! He has worked alone for so long."

"Alone except for you?" Father Hilario asked.

A slight lift of her heavy eyebrows suggested that she did not consider his remark in the best of taste.

"Except for my cousin and myself," she answered. "Naturally there are two of us."

"You are missionaries?"

"No, Father. We only serve."

"But Christians?"

"Of course."

As a priest, Father Hilario knew simplicity when he saw it. As a man of the world, he also recognized its dangers. It was quite possible for this thin, straight woman in, he supposed, her middle forties to belong to some curious sect which practiced polygamy. He remembered the strange, selfless aberrations of the Middle Ages, the calm bestialities of the seventeenth century and the odd privacies of modern prophets. He was careful to phrase his next question so that its meaning was not too definite.

"These women in white — are they the wives?"

"Oh, you have heard of them! How unexpected!"

She gave a professional laugh which, under the circumstances, sounded shameless.

"We have heard that Señor Carver has two hundred."

"That would be too many even for him, Father. At the moment he has eighty-nine."

The Diocesan Visitor stared into the tired, grayish face. Her reserved eyes might have belonged to a nun, and he was startled to find that he could not meet them.

"Who — who looks after this — er — family?" he asked uneasily.

"My cousin does. I care for the children."

"But is there not a — a chief wife, shall we say?"

"No, Father. We sell them when they are fifteen."

It was incredible. Heaven alone knew what mad heresy was at work among these defenseless Indians! The woman talked as if it were Christian and reasonable to have eighty-nine wives and sell them after . . . after . . . oh, ghastly thought!

Even Don Felipe, though not without a shade of envy, was shocked. He decided to test the matter immediately and beckoned to a smiling girl whose clumsy Indian figure was all turned to softness by her cotton sack.

"Are you a wife of the white man?" he asked.

"No. I was."

"You have a husband?"

"I am her husband," said a young man at her side.

He leaned upon his digging stick and regarded both his wife and Don Felipe with proud satisfaction.

"You like her?" inquired the administrator.

"Yes! White man's wives are the best! Many children! White man's wives . . ."

Don Felipe listened gravely to a flow of praise which would have been markedly indelicate in civilized society. The unnecessary details made it quite clear that girls who did not wear the white tunic were still sunk in the old tribal apathy, but that those who did wear it were enchanted by the attentions of husband and children.

He permitted himself to remember that his own private life in his river settlement was extremely unsatisfactory. If only one could get Father Hilario out of the way, a conversation with Don Salomón might be profitable. Yet he felt instinctively that Carver's transactions would be, in some way, far too individual to supply home comforts to lonely and deserving administrators.

"Señor Carver will be glad that you can talk to the Icuari," said the sister.

"You understand the language, too?"

"Naturally. I think Señor Carver would wish you to come with me now," she added.

"Magnificent! What patience! What devotion!" exclaimed Don Felipe to cover his embarrassment.

The track, graveled like a garden path where the slope was steep and the mud slippery, led them up the other side of the saddle and onto a considerable plateau. Its extent could only be guessed, for the climate was still warm enough and damp enough for the taste of the Icuari and for trees; but here and there the forest had been cut and the bogs primitively drained, leaving glades of desolate beauty.

As they entered the upper settlement, Carver, accompanied by a respectful retinue of men and women and the prancing gaieties of tiny children, came out to meet them. He had aged twenty years in nine, but was still recognizable: still a square, shortish man with a face like a hammered chunk of coarse-grained granite upon which some friend of the sculptor had drawn a burnt-cork mustache.

If he had been attired in a string instead of a shirt and trousers, his build, Don Felipe realized, would have been exactly that of the Indians. No doubt the appearance of common humanity had helped his success. He was neither too slim nor too tall to be unfamiliar.

"I must offer you my excuses. This friend" — Carver laid his hand on the shoulder of the guide — "should have brought you straight to us instead of coming first to ask for permission. I have never forgotten, Don Felipe, that it was you who allowed me to live here."

An odd reason for gratitude, you would think — to be allowed to die slowly of heat and mildew. But one grew to be content with little. What was Don Felipe himself but an underweight bag of bones and bacteria in a yellow skin?

He responded generously, quite conscious of his Spanish pleasure that there could be courtliness between two men at the world's end, and one of them dressed in rags.

"My distinguished friend! How should I not allow it? A man such as you wishing to study our country and its people! And now I have the honor to introduce to you Father Hilario, the representative of the bishop of the diocese."

"It is indeed an honor," said Carver, with a scrupulous bow.

"You are not, I believe, of the Church?" Father Hilario asked.

"Father, I fear the differences between one form of Christianity and another are — if I may say so without lack of respect — quite over the head of an anthropologist."

"But what, Don Salomón, do you teach?"

"I came here to learn, not to teach," Carver answered. "But I must admit my hand has been forced. We will speak of it later. You must be very hungry."

Father Hilario was — and the business of satisfying a stomach which had been three quarters empty for a week enabled him to control his indignation.

Under a leaf shelter Carver and his two guests squatted on stools before pots of food which was dully unpalatable by any civilized standard, but far more nourishing than that of the forest tribes. The plateau grew corn and four different kinds of potato. From the lower slopes the Icuari had bananas and a little coarse rice. Don Salomón apologized for the absence of meat. They killed occasional birds and deer, but it was impossible to keep meat for more than a day or two in their climate. He might, he said, have experimented with cattle if the clearings had not been just within the range of the vampire bat.

"But they do not look like a dying tribe now, would you say?" he asked proudly.

Sister Janet was passing the eating floor, trying — perhaps for the sake of Father Hilario — to look stern while being pulled apart by four-year-olds. In the middle distance Sheila, surrounded by half a dozen of the white-robed, was superintending a sinister caldron in which bones were being boiled for the manufacture of soap. The two cousins had a tendency to grow black hair — Janet between her eyebrows, Sheila upon her upper lip. Otherwise they had little in common, for Sheila, defying the climate, was bouncing and plump — a fit person, thought Father Hilario still scandalized in spite of a surfeit of potatoes, to seduce . . . to recruit . . . intolerable!

"How did you obtain these unfortunate Englishwomen, Don Salomón?" he asked.

"I knew them at home — from childhood almost. Trained governesses, they were. But nobody wants governesses any more. I wrote to them the very worst. Yes, I write and receive letters sometimes through my agent in Bolivia. But the worse I made it, the more they wished to come. So here they are. Unfortunate? Well, they do not think so, bless them! It compensates for a lot to see a people, naturally good, coming back day by day from death."

"No doubt you have been of much service to these innocents," said Father Hilario. "But I must know what doctrines you teach them."

Carver stared at him.

"Doctrines? I don't know. Ask Janet and Sheila! Ardent

Anglo-Catholics, they are. Not very different from your-
selves, I believe. I will try to make them take a day off if you
want to convert them. Takes longer than that, does it?
Well, no doubt they will meet you halfway."

The administrator, vaguely perceiving that there was no
common ground, returned the conversation to its point of
departure.

"You said you had brought them back from death, Don
Salomón?"

"Yes. There is no scientific justification. I am probably
quite wrong. But the Icuari had been very kind to me. So I
fear I forgot all my principles and settled down to raise the
birth rate. Fortunately I have a chance to show you how I
do it."

He called across the beaten earth of the village to the
sister whose plumpness suggested a far too easy conscience:

"Is the bride ready, Sheila?"

"Oh, yes, Mr. Carver! I think they are all waiting for you.
But hospitality comes first, doesn't it?" she added brightly.

Before Father Hilario could protest against the promised
spectacle, Carver had risen and carried his two guests along
with him. He stumped through the huts like a solid captain
proud of his quarter-deck and entered a crowd of the Icuari
which parted to let him through. The casual, contented
movement was far more impressive than respect.

Under a shelter of boughs were standing a girl in a white
tunic, a young potbellied savage with an immense navel and
a wide grin, and what presumably were their families. Four
old men squatted in a corner, wise, naked and unconcerned.

They were the color of rotten pineapples and had something of the same smell.

"Would you care to do a professional job on these two children, Padre?" Carver invited.

The Diocesan Visitor did not reply. His set face was sufficient answer.

"Very well, then, I shall carry on as usual. I assure you that you have no reason to object if Janet and Sheila do not. They have approved my translation of the marriage service into Icuari."

"Then you do teach — all three of you!"

"I know. I should not do it. But it was unavoidable. Let me give you an example. The Icuari believe that maternal uncles become armadillos after death. That is of great interest. But once I had noted every aspect of any value to anthropology, I found the belief as inconvenient as they did. Defunct maternal uncles are a social nuisance. So I just outlined as much Christianity as a child of five could be expected to assimilate."

"A child of five," exclaimed Father Hilario, "is not too young to be corrupted."

"Really, Father, you are most narrow-minded. We cannot possibly do better until you send us a missionary. Now, we are going to approve the price of the bride first."

Don Felipe swallowed a last mouthful and stuffed half a potato into his pocket. His power over both contestants was in theory absolute — though in practice limited by a sincere desire to avoid trouble either with the Icuari or with the Church — but he was aware that during the collision of such characters a civil servant would be wise to confine himself to his daily bread.

It was safe and proper, however, to put on the paternal face which he used for official occasions. Judicially and with his finger tips together, he heard the bridegroom declare that six poles of seasoned wood, sheltered from rain and free of white ant, were offered for the bride.

Carver turned to the four old men.

"Am I to accept the six poles?"

They made a solemn pretense of consulting one another, but it was plain to Don Felipe that the committee's decision had been reached, much as elsewhere, before the formal meeting.

"It is too cheap. He must add a roof beam."

"You hear?"

"I will add a roof beam."

The bride's expression turned from slight anxiety to pride. She had cost her husband — considering his tools — months of patience and hard work.

During the ceremony Father Hilario kept silence, for it was simple and reverent. There could be no doubt that this heretic and his two women, however abominable their doctrine, had accustomed the Icuari to Christian ritual. It was not until dancing and drinking began and the laity — if one could think of them as laity — had reverted to their primeval paganism that he demanded:

"Was that woman your wife, or was she not?"

"By tribal law she was," Carver replied.

"And how long has she been so?"

"Sheila, how long was she my wife?"

"You bought her from her uncle when she was eight. Number Forty-seven on the card index. A very obstinate case of worms. You ought to remember, Mr. Carver," said Sheila sternly. "I do not know how you got on at all before Janet and I came."

Don Salomón for the first time looked slightly embarrassed.

"It's the bad habit of trusting to your cards," he said. "Of course! Comes back to me now. Pretty little thing, she was. She came in on that bad lot of skins. They rotted in six months. Shocking! I had to pay for her all over again."

"With what kind of skins?" asked Don Felipe politely.

"Otter. The price of a wife is nine skins. Quite understandable. A mink coat, as it were. A very sound medium of exchange originally."

"Sound, in heaven's name!" Father Hilario exclaimed.

"Originally, I said. When the Icuari were a river people it was a practical form of dowry. It proved that the bridegroom had enterprise and could handle a canoe. But after they migrated to these valleys they found few otters, and soon wiped those out. To get nine otter skins took years of hunting. And by the time the last was collected, ants or mildew had usually destroyed the first. A man like that" — he pointed to the aggressively dancing bridegroom — "had no hope of a wife till he was so old that he would care for nothing but sitting round a fire.

"That was the position when they received me as their guest. Too little money chasing too many goods. Result —

no children. We are all conservative in these matters. The Icuari would not change from otter skins any more than we will change from gold."

"And so you took advantage of that?" asked Don Felipe with an entirely neutral courtesy.

"Yes. There was nothing else for it. I gave a standing order for otter skins in Bolivia. No one else wants them. My agent thinks I am mad. But he collects them for me, and I go and fetch them twice a year."

"But then you do not leave any wives for anyone else!"

"Oh, that's an exaggeration! But whenever I find a promising child with no hope of a husband, I marry her myself and sell her when she is fit to be sold."

Don Felipe was ashamed of his past inactivity. What an exposure of his liberal administration! And under the horrified eyes of the Church!

"This passing through your hands enhances their value?" he asked.

"No! No! No!" answered Carver with forced academic patience. "It reduces their value. That's the whole point. As a man of the world, you should understand it at once."

The Anglo-Saxon shamelessness of the man was distasteful to Don Felipe. Any truly Christian gentleman would have clothed such a remark in more decent ambiguity.

"And how did you — to use a frank expression — get away with it?"

"Simple, once I had their confidence! Night after night with the old men. There they are! Just like politicians anywhere else — walking memories, but no constructive thought for the future! Chatter, chatter. I took it all down. Rivers flowing and maternal uncles, and quiet acceptance that the tribe must die. And then they came out with the tale of a custom permitting a husband to sell his wife for anything he liked to take. Quite legal, but half forgotten. Naturally! Who would want to sell a wife when it was practically impossible to buy one?

Well, I saw my way at once. I could buy them young for otter skins and sell them for something sensible when they were fifteen. That is what you have just seen me do — sell a wife for the makings of a sound hut. I shall put the married couple in it, of course."

"I have a liberal education," exclaimed Don Felipe. "No one can say I do not sympathize with temptation. But eighty-nine!"

"Yes, it's astonishing how my little family grew. I taught them a bit of sensible religion and tried to give them self-respect. Any man can handle a girl up to the age of eleven or so. But time passes. When my first batch of wives were close on twelve, I had to send for Janet and Sheila."

"It is beyond belief!" Don Felipe cried, all the more angry because he was aware of a most improper jealousy. "And then to introduce two crazed women to assist you!"

Carver stood up and, instantly, the old men with him.

"What the devil do you mean, man? Crazed women — those two angels? Come out of here immediately!"

The Icuari had perceived his anger. Don Felipe realized that they would strike out like frightened children if Carver made the least gesture of violence, but had a human faith that Carver would not. After all, he himself had sometimes been in a position to raise a finger. He scurried through the dancers a little ahead of his host, endeavoring to preserve an expression of the utmost geniality.

The Diocesan Visitor followed more slowly, smiling with inexplicable tenderness. He even blessed the bride as he passed her. It was extremely unfair, Don Felipe thought, that Father Hilario should leave the secular authority to interrogate this disgraceful debauchee and then shy away from the results. Typical of those black crows, it was! The Church, to start with, had been altogether too ready to bring in its thunders and, having made all the trouble, was now being exquisitely courteous.

"Don Salomón," Father Hilario was saying, "you have been in the forest how long?"

"Let me see now! Crazed women indeed! Let me see! A year before I found the Icuari. And six — no, no, over eight years since."

"Verily, what devotion! No wonder it was difficult at first for us to understand each other."

"I cannot see why. Souls for God, you want, don't you? Well — if I may use your terminology — when I began to love these people, so did I. Increase and multiply, that is what I am trying to make them do. Clear, I hope? Many thanks! No reason for a government officer to think we are all mad, is there? Look at that!"

Sister Janet, attended by two nursery maids in the white tunic of Carver's wives, was telling a story to a dozen or so fascinated infants.

"*Suffer little children to come unto Me,*" Carver explained.

"I ought not to allow it. It is gross interference with their own folklore. But the fact is, Padre, I have found in practice that if you want to raise a whole community from the dead, there is nothing like elementary Christianity to do it."

"That has been our experience, too," said Father Hilario gravely. "I am very glad to hear it confirmed from such an — unexpected quarter. May I inspect the children, Sister?"

"Of course, Reverend Padre," Janet replied proudly. "Their heads are beautifully clean now."

Don Felipe, left out of the conversation in disgrace, also looked closely at the Icuari nursery class. He knew what Father Hilario was up to. Either of them, from long experience, could distinguish as little as one eighth of white blood. There was none.

He ventured to reassert himself with a delicate question:

"Sister Janet, the bride whom we have just seen married — would you describe her as . . . well . . . inexperienced?"

"Certainly not, Don Felipe. She was one of my best pupils."

The administrator blinked his fever-yellowed eyes under the impact of such innocence, but tried again.

"And you see nothing questionable in this second marriage?"

"No, Don Felipe. After all, they are quite normal girls. They would be very disappointed if they had to belong to Mr. Carver's family forever, wouldn't they?"

Father Hilario opened his arms in a jovial gesture which included the desolate, rain-sodden hilltop and all the children, old and young, upon it. His bark of laughter sounded through Icuari mists the sunlit trumpets of Europe.

"What's up? What's amusing you?" asked Carver suspiciously.

"My dear noble friend! Ah, but you must see the jest of it!"

"I do not," Don Salomón insisted formally. "You must forgive me. The Icuari laugh seldom. One loses the habit."

Don Felipe silently agreed. It was appallingly true — poor devils that they were out there in the uninhabitable. He himself, before this journey with Father Hilario, had for years seen no reason for any more than a melancholy smile.

"You have never any thought of the world outside — you and your two angels?"

"I must admit, Padre, there are times when we think of home. But what with keeping each other alive and speaking the language to each other, we do tend to become single-minded — indeed, apart from our purpose, to have few thoughts the Icuari cannot share."

"But they would not mind, I suppose," Father Hilario asked, "if the girls you buy were your wives in fact as well as name?"

"Mind? No, of course they wouldn't. Oh, I understand at last! Laughing at yourself, were you? The inquisitor descending upon Bluebeard! But, my dear fellow, it beats me that you couldn't see from your own experience how that sort of thing interferes with a mission."

The administrator gasped at so uncompromising a rejection of opportunity.

"If you had any faith, Don Salomón, you would be a saint!" he protested.

"Don Felipe," said Father Hilario, "when God has produced the miracle before the faith, we should not, I think, be too ready to advise Him from our own experiments in mere trifles of administration which should come first and which second."

The Eye of a Soldier

THE older I get, the more I see that it is trust between man and man which keeps civilization together. You wondered just now how I stand the strain of commanding on the Syrian frontier. And I must admit that Caesar has graciously given me more responsibility than troops.

Tell him we are alert, but not alarmed. I have the confidence of the Parthian governor across the border, and between the pair of us we settle any frontier incidents. A much more able general than I am, he can do what he likes with his home government. As soon as I realized that, I set myself to win his friendship.

If the fates send you a man worthy of trust, then trust him — that has always been my principle! I will give you a very odd instance. It happened twenty years ago. Do you remember Silvanus? Yes, that one — a possible for color sergeant if only he had been tall enough. Now there's a man who has left a beloved memory behind him!

You were at Caesarea then with the legion, and I was commanding the detachment of instructors which we had lent to Herod Antipas to train his local levies. A delicate job for any centurion, even of my seniority! But it was no use sending Herod a battalion commander. Except for the very few who have come up the hard way, like ourselves, they never know anything about drill.

We made a handy little force of the levies, too — just as fast as the Arab raiders and twice as efficient. Lack of discipline always means so much unnecessary bloodshed.

I often wonder how much it was all due to Silvanus. I should never have persuaded him to come with me if he hadn't been feeling mutinous because the pay was cut. He was just a loyal, sturdy Italian peasant who might have gone far if only he could have bothered to learn to read and write. As it was, a proper old soldier, wise as an owl and not above feathering his nest! The gods know he needed it! But a man on whom his centurion could utterly rely. You know how fond of them one gets.

Of course my handful of instructors thought themselves Romans among barbarians when they first arrived, and I saw that Silvanus sweated the wine out of them on an early parade in our own barracks before turning them loose on recruits. Meanwhile I made it my business to learn Aramaic in order to keep the lot of them out of trouble.

They looked for it sometimes. At Capernaum there was a beautiful little grove with its own stream, set just where the blue spearhead of Lake Tiberias would join the shaft, which they insisted was the perfect site for a temple to Jupiter.

I quite agreed with them. But it could not possibly be allowed. Jews are absurdly sensitive about what they call graven images. You remember all the excitement when Pilate carried the Eagles into Jerusalem — a first-class revolt on his hands in twenty-four hours! Myself, I used to warn the villagers whenever there was a color party marching up the Damascus road from Caesarea, so that they could look the other way. And they did — all but the small boys, of course.

Well, the main point was that there should be some sort of worship on a site which was made for it, and my fellows were not fussy about the various aspects of Jove. So I asked the headman of Capernaum if they would take over the services of a temple themselves and dedicate it to their own Jupiter. Rather like Plato's God, if I understood it — who must exist, but a simple soul like mine needs an intermediary. They were delighted, and so were my instructors. We had a couple of army surveyors with us, training road foremen, and it was child's play for them to run up a temple from the priest's drawings, though it looked a bit bare to me when it was finished.

After that we were as popular as a foreign military mission can ever hope to be. The local population used to talk to me about their history and religion — which seemed one and the same thing — and take me to visit their schools of wisdom. I made very little of it all, but I did learn to feel the mystery behind the words.

One summer evening several of my friends rowed me over to the east shore of the lake to listen to a philosopher who was making a considerable stir by his healing and his curious doctrines. They were doubtful about his politics, and I think they may have wanted me to question him. He was sitting by the side of a goat track and talking to some fishermen. I listened for half an hour, or more. Once our eyes met, and he smiled at me. But I had no right to speak.

I cannot describe him to you at all. You know what every

intelligent man thinks when he worships Caesar as a god — that he could never have been such a master of his own luck unless he were as much above plain mortals as the gods are. So was this philosopher compared to ordinary men. He was divine. But his gold was the dust haze of the road, and his purple the bare hills in the last of the sun. He made me believe that law and the sword are only a beginning, and that the true virtue in making order is to prepare the way for gentleness and pity. I tell you he was young and lovely as Apollo in the stories of the Golden Age.

Soon after that Silvanus got his last attack of marsh fever. A shocking place for it, the Jordan Valley! I saw that he obeyed the doctor's orders to stay off the low ground, but it made no difference. The disease kept on coming back. And when hemorrhage set in, the doctor said Silvanus had had it. A clever Greek he was, true to his Hippocratic oath and excellent on wounds. Provided you could crawl off the field at all, you had a good chance of recovery.

If Silvanus had just been indispensable, I do not think I could have done what I did. But I loved the man; and that, I felt, gave me the right to call in the Galilean philosopher. When you appealed to him for the right reason he would heal. Never for show, or for money.

Of course I asked our Greek first. He called the cures harmless witchcraft which was efficacious when a man felt ill and wasn't, and of no use at all in a case of acute marsh fever.

Sound medical theory, no doubt. Yet I believe that if you feel ill you are, and healing is just as mysterious whether it is marsh fever or a Parthian spear in your liver or thinking you are Cincinnatus at the full moon. Somewhere is a divine law which we do not understand.

I did not like to ask the Galilean to come to my quarters, where Silvanus was lying. I had a bust of Grandfather up, and a *Roma Dea* and my delightful little bronze Aphrodite from Alexandria. Not that I thought he would have objected. But I hate putting people in a false position.

So I wrote him one of those flowery Oriental letters which all Syrians understand, saying that I was not worthy to receive him but that I should much appreciate a word from him about Silvanus.

And just to be on the safe side, I asked a delegation of my Capernaum friends to carry the letter, as I knew they would tell him all about the temple, and that for a Roman centurion I was a reasonable companion. Myself, I doubted if any of this ceremoniousness was necessary. Apollo would not expect you to carry on like the court jeweler trying to get something on account out of Herod Antipas.

Having made all the proper gestures, I walked down the valley to see him myself. I left my uniform at home. I knew he would not be impressed by it. As a matter of fact, I do not think his own followers had any clear idea who I was. They were not interested in Rome.

And then a second time I looked into his eyes. It was as one soldier to another, as if I were saluting Caesar. You know the feeling. There you are, a very small part of the world and yet in contact with all of it. But, as I have tried to tell you, he had an utterly different kind of greatness. We were not in Caesar's world.

I told him about Silvanus, and how I loved the man.

"You need not go out of your way, sir," I said. "Just — do it."

"What makes you think I can?" he asked.

I am very bad at explaining myself. But I had a sense that what I said would, in some strange way, matter — matter more, I mean, than even words of mine which could now compel life or death on the frontier.

"Because there is a law in life as in the legion," I answered, "and you, sir, know what it is. I give an order. I say to a man Go, and he goes; or Come, and he comes. I do not have to be present to see that the order is carried out. Nor do you."

"Go back," he said. "Your servant is healed."

And then he turned to the crowd which had collected, and told them he had not seen such faith in all the Jews.

I do not understand what he meant to this day. I have no faith at all. I am a professional soldier, not a priest. But I know the power to command when I see it, and who was I to impose any limit upon his?

I shall never forget him. I cannot help recognizing that he must have gone to his death as willingly as you would or I, provided we knew it our duty to civilization — though, speaking for myself, if I foresaw that pain was going to be as cruel as upon the cross I should think twice about it. Yes, he was crucified by Pilate.

Children's Crusade

HE FOUND it hard to believe that Israel was as welcoming to every tourist. His host, Joseph Horsha, was a mere professor of history, internationally known but not so distinguished that he could lay down an invisible red carpet for any Englishman who happened to be staying in his house. Looking out over the glittering Mediterranean from the top of Carmel and green shade, Mayne's sense of well-being was near perfect, yet faintly disturbed by the suspicion that he was the subject of gossip, that everyone — Horsha, this Ben Aron woman and even the taxi driver who had brought her — knew something which he did not.

Aviva Ben Aron claimed mysteriously to have met him before, though he was quite certain she was wrong. A most exceptional woman. Calm — that had been his impression of her during lunch. Not a quality you would expect from an overworked Undersecretary of State in a new and sensitive country. It was as if she had had some experience — a superb love affair, perhaps — which gave her enough pity and self-confidence to last a lifetime.

"And all this time you have never been in Israel, when it was Palestine?" she asked.

"No. Only looked at it from afar, like Moses. I was a

soldier in Egypt then. Thirty-five years ago. And, Lord, how young!"

"Gloriously young!" she answered, smiling.

"Now, just what is this attractive mystery?" he demanded. "Where did we meet?"

"I was one of the children, Mr. Mayne — one of the twenty-six."

It was like all his memories of the first war, vanished if he were alone, vivid the instant some sharer recalled them. At once he was back on the quays of Port Said, the dust blowing, the crowd of diseased and powerful Egyptian laborers laughing at a crane as it dumped on the wharf dead and dying horses from the holds of a cattle ship which had met bad weather in the Indian Ocean. The sterile, vulgarian sun pointed the details of every dried and eddying patch of filth; and meanwhile the smart Italian freighter glided to her berth with twenty-six boys and girls leaning over the rails and staring with excited eyes at the hideous Orient as if it were the gate of heaven.

He had not recognized the pattern of the future. At the end of that first and, to civilians, kindlier war there had been no need of any elaborate organization to deal with refugees and displaced persons. The Middle East had few, and those belonging to obscure and persecuted Christian sects — simple souls whose problems could be solved by the loan of a donkey to carry their baggage. As for Zionists, nobody in 1919, outside political circles, had ever heard of them. In dealing with these astonishing Jewish children, who ought to have been in school and wanted to go to Palestine, Mayne had no precedent at all to follow.

The naval authorities and the Egyptian police had passed the muddle to him, for it was obvious that the children, if allowed to land, would become the responsibility of the military government. Mayne was the Port Control Officer. What he decided would be, for the time being, accepted. He had been well aware of his exact value to his superiors: a man who knew his own mind, saved everyone trouble and was sufficiently unimportant to be sacrificed if anything went wrong.

He went up to the captain's cabin under the bridge to see what the devil this Italian thought he was about. The fellow's enthusiasm annoyed him. It appeared that the children had made an overwhelming impression upon his emotional people; but twenty-six young lunatics from unknown depths of Central Europe, with the sketchiest of papers and very little money, couldn't just be dumped on the Port Said waterfront while a rapturous captain sailed back to Italy, rubbing his hands with easy satisfaction at a good deed done.

Under the circumstances a blaze of Latin oratory was impertinent. Mayne refused to allow the children to land and posted a solid pair of sentries at the foot of the gangway.

"You had not the slightest idea of the difficulties," he said, the memory of the day and the Italian captain adding a hardness to his voice.

"It never even occurred to us that there were any," Joseph Horsha replied.

"Were you with them too, Jo? Why have you never told me?"

"Look — it was as if we had both assisted at some secret, sacred ceremony. Something to remember, not to talk of. And when we met again so many years later, I couldn't tell whether you recognized me or not. The silences of Englishmen are so effective. One has to respect them."

Mayne searched his vague memory of the children whose eyes had followed him so gaily and confidently as he went ashore to put his sentries on the gangway. There had been five girls, more stern than attractive. Perhaps that was to be expected. A girl who preferred such a mad pilgrimage to the enthralling adventure of becoming a woman was bound to lack the charm of adolescence — or rather to have ripened her character before her emotions. That would account for the gray-haired, classical grace of Aviva Ben Aron. The foundation of her was indeed a love affair — though not in the generally accepted sense.

The boys — well, of course the quest itself had singled them out. It was impossible that any boy capable of starting and finishing such an adventure should not have the face of a dreamer. They looked like young Galahads, like any sentimental Victorian engraving of ardent youth. The oddness of some of the faces — to his Gentile eye — simply didn't count. If Joseph had been one of those boys, his whole warm character was still in keeping. The blade of youth, now sharpened down to a more serviceable flexibility, was set forever into his lean, sensitive features and the eagerness of his mind.

"My name then was Joseph Wald. Horsha is the Hebrew translation."

"Wald, of course! A fiery little scamp you were!"

"Not rude, I hope?"

"None of you was ever rude. You had no need to be. You knew you were irresistible."

"That was really the impression we gave?" Aviva Ben Aron asked. "I'm glad I didn't spoil it. I was just fifteen — and an imaginative little girl."

"You weren't afraid?" Horsha asked incredulously.

"Wasn't I? To be put ashore in Port Said with no protection but you visionary male children . . ."

Perhaps those two round-faced, Midland sentries at the foot of the brow had been justified after all, Mayne thought. To the girls, at any rate, rifle and bayonet couldn't have been half so frightening as all those evil Egyptian faces. After all the years he was still offended at the Italian lack of common sense in proposing to sling overboard, like so much cargo, twenty-six starry-eyed children.

"You leave the Italians alone," Horsha told him. "Responsibility is your forte. Emotional sympathy is theirs."

"One does expect some sanity all the same."

"No! Sanity would have been out of place in dealing with us. We had made our own world, where sanity didn't exist at all."

The conspiracy, Horsha explained, had run through the high schools of Cracow like a childish epidemic. No one knew who started it; no one could tell who would resist it. Those who went down with the highest fever had been the least Jewish of Jews. That wasn't surprising. The submerged and the religious had not yet assimilated the Balfour Declaration. To them it was just another prophecy, not an immediate invitation to act.

He told of his own romantic concept as precisely as if it had been read rather than lived. His family had been cultured Poles. The medieval courts of the legends had been as familiar to him as the court of King Solomon, and morally preferable. That had been true — though perhaps in a lesser degree — for most of his companions as well.

Their Zionism was the natural flower of Christian chivalry and Jewish tradition, owing nothing at all to propaganda. A last crusade had driven the Turks from Jerusalem. A statesman of the conquerors had declared that Palestine was open to the Jews. The facts did not belong to the modern world; they were gay and stirring as the summoning song of a minstrel. What gesture could one make in answer but to put up the Star of David upon an imaginary shield, and march?

At the first secret meeting there might have been a hundred boys and girls, aged from twelve to seventeen. When the cautious had weeded themselves out, thirty were left. They came from respectable, conventional families, but the ebb and flow of war had destroyed their natural fear of movement. Soldiers in thousands tramped over Europe, seeking their legitimate or spiritual homes. Therefore children could do the same, all the way to Palestine.

They even called themselves Crusaders, without any sense of incompatibility with their Jewish traditions. Who could refuse to let them pass, provided that their voluntary dedication was plainly to be seen?

In the privacy of a ruined factory belonging to Horsha's parents they took their solemn vows — to be honorable in all their dealings, to protect the weak, to preserve chastity. That final promise, though at their age not hard to fulfill, seemed to them the most important. It was an echo not so much of saintliness as of the precepts of parents.

"It's unbelievable that we could have been so cruel to them," Aviva said.

"Birds leave the nest."

"Yes. You used that argument then. It sounded as if it meant something."

"We did warn them," Joseph protested, still with the guilty laugh of a boy.

Yes — and the parents had given parental and understanding replies. Of course the children, if they were sure, quite sure, they wanted it, could go to Palestine as soon as education was finished, as soon as the routes were open, as soon as arrangements could be made to receive them. Fathers and mothers could well afford to be sympathetic. Travel was manifestly impossible till the aftermath of war had been cleared.

But instinctively the children knew that only in a time of unrest could their crusade succeed. The world which they had imagined was close to reality. That casual, medieval society which endured for months before frontiers were formally re-established had little interest in stopping the determined traveler.

Horsha and Aviva Ben Aron, both talking at once as if they had eagerly returned to childhood, tumbled incident upon incident. The children had kept their secret profoundly well. They bought and hid packs and water bottles, and put their money, collected by small economies and the naïve, ingenious tricks of the young, into a common store. They chose for their departure the early morning of a day when there was no school, and said — for they were determined not to start with a lie — that they were off on an expedition, that they didn't know when they would be back and that they promised all to keep together. The smallest, in much need of comfort, remembered the hundreds of boys who had enlisted well under military age without telling their parents.

So fathers and mothers, patient for a whole day and three quarters of a night, discovered at last, like burghers of Hamelin, that their children had vanished and did not even guess, till a joint telegram arrived, what piper had summoned them. Meanwhile the thirty had pushed their way among peasants and demobilized soldiers from train to crowded train, and were beyond recall.

The two frontiers which they crossed were still hardly delineated, and officials easily allowed them to pass through to Vienna. They were subjects of the Austro-Hungarian Empire, and their identity cards were in order. It was nobody's business to hold them for inquiries.

But also it was nobody's business to send them back. The urgent requests of the Cracow police were presumably dropped into trays marked PENDING. Austrians who were going to remain Austrians and Austrians who were going to be Czechs had no interest in the problems of Austrians who were going to be Poles. Children bursting with health and excitement on their way to Palestine? Good luck to them! It would be time enough to bother if the Italians refused to let them pass.

At Vienna they bought several days' supply of bread and sausage, and used the last of their money to travel clear of the too curious city and its suburbs. When they got off the train they were as destitute as all the saintly beggars of history. That, indeed, was high adventure for the sake of their quest. They felt at last free. Confident and singing, they began their march over the mountain roads towards the Italian frontier two hundred miles away.

Aviva laughed like a girl at the memory.

"I've never been so sure in my life that what I was doing was right — unsurpassably right!" she said. "And ever since, when I think my conscience is happy, I have been able to test it by that day."

"We were giving joy, too," Joseph added. "I don't think any of us realized it then. We just assumed that the world was as good as the first day God made it. But to the villagers we were the return of joy and innocence after four years of war. It was enough for them to see our faces. They gave us barns and sometimes their beds to sleep in. They showered us with milk and food."

"And wine," said Aviva. "How inhuman little male saints can be!"

"No, no! You never understood. It was essential that our spirit should not be lost — that nothing should be dissipated."

"I don't know what you're talking about," Mayne reminded them.

"One of our sixteen-year-olds got drunk," Aviva explained.

"The other boys court-martialed him and sent him home — or rather back to Vienna, where he fortunately had an uncle. The mayor of the village lent him money for his fare."

The mayor had done his best for the offender, too. Drunkenness wasn't such a crime, he told the children. Why, before the war the dear *Wandervögel* were often merry in the evening! Yes, he understood that they had set themselves a religious standard, but didn't the boy's shame count with them?

It did not. The young faces regarded advocate and criminal with blank severity. They knew they were right. Horsha still declared that they were right. They were following, quite blindly, a European tradition. Only that tradition, reflected in their joy and their purity of manners and living, could carry the pilgrims through to the Holy Land.

As they drew nearer to the frontier, they were told again and again that the Italians would never let them through. The Italians, said the sentimental Austrians, were not in the least like themselves. The children would meet the victors in full flush of insolence. And what of girls of fifteen and sixteen unprotected among Latins?

The whole countryside was fascinated by their march, and in committee for their welfare. It was considered that they would appear to have some official backing if they crossed the Julian Alps by rail; so friendly railway men gave them a lift in a goods train over the pass, and unloaded the twenty-nine on the frontier station.

"You must have felt pretty forlorn then," said Mayne.

No, Joseph insisted, they had not. But possibly their faces showed enough anxiety to make them appear as suppliants

— enough to prevent the feeling in any sensitive official that his beloved frontier was about to be ravished against its will.

The children's unity of purpose was such that it had never occurred to them to elect or appoint a leader. But the Latin mind demanded a leader. One couldn't talk with twenty-nine children at the same time — that was reasonable, wasn't it? It was indeed, though to the children the problem was how to explain themselves at all when eight Italians were talking at once. At last there was no sound in the mountain silence but the hissing of the locomotive. The utter improbability of the situation had imposed itself.

Those kindly Italians! A sergeant of Bersaglieri laid his hand upon the shoulder of the youngest, choosing him as spokesman. He was twelve and looked, after the hardships of the journey, no more than ten. The sergeant questioned him in bad German, while the frontier officials, instantly appreciating this paternal gesture, gathered round them.

The boy spoke up boldly. Money? No, they hadn't any. Was it then so important? They had reached Italy without it, and so they could reach Palestine.

But the sea? Hadn't one to cross the sea to go to Palestine?

Yes, certainly, said the twelve-year-old spokesman, surer of his geography than the sergeant. The English who had promised them the land and who had so many ships would provide.

Italian imagination, swift to identify itself with generosity, assumed its part in promise and victory alike. Had not Italy ships? Had not Italy, too, been engaged against the

Turks? And was it not a historic occasion, this arrival of pilgrim children on their frontier?

"It was you, I remember, who put that point to them, Aviva."

"Yes. I felt it so strongly that I found myself stammering it all out in spite of shyness. I was sure that we were the first of many — the first, that is, to go in a body to a Palestine that was ours again. How right children are and how absurd! A little big-eyed prophet telling the commander of an Italian frontier post that the eyes of history were on him!"

It had been enough, at any rate, for the commander to spread his wings and send a wire to Venice. Meanwhile the children, no longer laughing but still confident that these excitable strangers could not refuse them, were herded into the barracks by the friendly sergeant and given two empty rooms — a large one for the boys, a smaller for the girls.

That was their worst night. They made their first acquaintance with hungry bugs. They remembered the warnings of the Austrian peasants. Crusading gallantry rose to the occasion. Horsha and his bosom friend slept on the bare boards of the passage outside the girls' door, and awoke to find the licentious Italian soldiery tenderly tiptoeing about their military business with bare feet in order not to disturb them.

The following afternoon came a reply, permitting the Polish children who claimed to be Jews to be sent down to Venice.

"Our frontier friends couldn't have put it better," said Horsha ironically. "Polish children who claim to be Jews sound much more sympathetic than Jewish children who claim to be Poles."

"And all that is over for us!" Aviva exclaimed. "All finished by the name Israeli!"

They caught the imagination of a people. The newspapers christened their march a new Children's Crusade. The great, grave Jewish-Italian families took them to their bosoms.

"You can't imagine how we were feted — and how it seemed somehow to spoil all the beautiful simplicity!"

Even the Church was fascinated, and held up the children as examples of the conduct to be expected of Christians as well. But Christian children, who had no comparable objective, only felt that self-discipline when presented as adventure was a fraud. What it was really worthwhile to imitate they understood. Parties, armed with axes and their fathers' carving knives, set out in stolen boats to conquer Fiume or Africa, and were brought home weeping. The Church quietly and decisively moved the pilgrims on to Rome.

At Rome it was harder still to preserve their common flame. By letters they were in touch at last with parents, and their proud sense of isolation was disturbed by remittances of money and loving reproaches. Then the Roman matrons put out as well the light of chivalry by separating girls from boys. To march singing across the foothills of the Alps had been easy. The journey through Vanity Fair was a more searching test.

The boys insisted on remaining together. Their dormitory was the vast empty salon of a palace, where the neat beds were lined against marble walls like insignificant white mice. Only their impatience saved them from being extinguished. To go on. That was all they wanted — to go on. Their hosts, though ravished by their innocent courage, found them obstinate and insensitive.

One of the girls fell in love and became engaged to be married — as young as Juliet and just as ecstatic. They thought this an indecency, plain evidence of the approaching moral rot. And then the eldest of them, a few months over seventeen, was led astray by the daughter of a Jewish family which was great but not so grave.

If he had confessed, he might have been expelled with dignity. But he boasted.

"We flung him out," said Horsha savagely, "flung him out with everything that belonged to him!"

"They had to keep their illusions," Aviva explained in half apology. "Illusion was the driving force."

"I had no idea that the girls were not in full sympathy," Joseph Horsha remarked, still with the remains of disquiet from thirty-five years before.

"We were. But it was such a relief in Rome, for a little while, not to have to play your game. Attachments had grown, you see — all very innocent and romantic."

"Not with any of us!"

She did not answer. But even if a few of the little warriors were being civilized in secret by their ladies, there was no deflecting either from their purpose. The Roman matrons found their pets untamable, and dismissed them with the magnificent gesture of a free passage to Egypt.

Presumably some diplomat, general or influential prince

was ordered to approach the British authorities. He may indeed have written; but, if he did, his letter was slipped into some file reserved for the improbable and impossible. Palestine did not yet exist, only a Syria about to be divided between French and British. There was no government but the staff of Allenby's army, sorting out, with brusque military common sense, the unfamiliar complexities of Turkish administration.

At Genoa twenty-six children, overjoyed to be again together and in movement, went on board the freighter and down to a baggage room which had been roughly partitioned for the boys and girls, and furnished with camp beds. Of the original thirty, one was to be married, two had been guilty of unknightly behavior, and a fourth had died in Italy of influenza. They couldn't have said what on earth they expected to find on arrival: turbaned Turks, perhaps, or even some modern remnant of Pharaoh's linen-kilted courtiers — certainly not an impersonal military organization, with its Captain Maynes and its sentries blandly unaffected by any crusade but their own.

After the first hours of looking down from the deck upon Port Said, excitement lost its edge. Not even imagination was justified. True, there were palms and sand. But Egyptians did not ride camels; they unloaded dead horses and loaded coal. Where were the glittering caravans of the Orient, and the British cavalry which had ridden to Jerusalem? Where the curiosity or enmity that their arrival should have occasioned? The heroes of Balfour and Allenby were red-faced, red-kneed soldiers, wearing ridiculous shorts like very little boys. They entered things in notebooks and bawled at the

Egyptians instead of clinking their sabers magnificently up
and down the quay. This busy world had nothing in common
with kindly Europe, continuous, in spite of varying scenery
and manners, from Cracow to Rome.

During the morning all action was inhibited. Outside the
refuge of the ship's awnings the sun smote dishearteningly
upon stone and iron. The strange inhabitants of the quay
continued to work. The Italian captain was fuming and unapproachable. British naval and military officers came and
went, passing the eager group with noncommittal smiles.

Then the spirit of the crusade reasserted itself. There was
a moment's talk, and the children picked up their packs,
without any order given or any formal agreement among
them, and marched together down the gangway. They ignored the casual request to hop it and the subsequent sharp
command to halt. Nor was the sentry's bayonet in itself de-
cisive.

The bayonet belonged in their world — which, after all,
contained the possibility of martyrdom, though no chance of
it had yet appeared. But while the boys hesitated before that
unwavering point at the foot of the gangway the sentry's
companion gave them a broad grin and a wink, and with a
jerk of the thumb dismissed them. His confidence was un-
shakable as their own, and his friendly gesture intelligible;
it pointed out that the bayonet was not really sharp steel but
merely a wall, an unclimbable wall, around the stately park
of empire. The irresistible force had met the immovable object.

"And in the end there is no way out of that," Aviva said,
"but to learn to hate."

"No, you can't find parallels," Horsha went on. "There aren't any. The British, as they were in 1919 — yes, and later — had the art of making the rest of the world feel ashamed of impatience. That sentry — with his tiny private share of it — was quite enough for twenty-six crusaders."

Thereafter the slow mass of bureaucracy crept over and engulfed them. Up and down that gangway, to them forbidden, passed the Egyptian police, the port authorities, the Italian consul and the agent of the line. From the conferences in the saloon the Italians emerged profane and glowering, the English unyielding and self-satisfied; and all of them combined to make the children appear in their own eyes young nuisances rather than young heroes. But never did it occur to them that they were unreasonable, or that their knightliness could be defeated. Hardest of all to bear was the young army captain, Mayne, who spoke in courtly French quite intelligible to the high school students, and merely seemed to be amused.

"You didn't mind the general," Mayne protested. "He was just as amused as I."

"We were good Polish citizens," Joseph answered. "We treated generals with respect. And he understood us. A man who isn't a boy at heart can never become a general. Half his job is to persuade men that they are really having the marvelously exciting time they dreamed of when they were twelve."

"It wasn't till much later," explained Aviva, "that we realized you had brought the general yourself."

Well, of course, he had. And it was true that he had been amused — delighted was a better word — by the glorious folly of the pilgrimage. He was surprised to find himself most reluctant to have the children's fire put out by a great wad of paper, or to return them to Italy. His sentries, as a precaution, were correct; as a solution, they were intolerable.

He persuaded the general to take the children off the ship and, pending a decision, to send them down the Suez Canal to a camp at Kantara. The old professional had been impressed by their quality — by their tremendous button-polishing capacity if they had any buttons. All the same, he insisted, some inexpensive method of returning them to Poland would have to be found. It was impossible to allow them into Palestine, utterly impossible.

"He didn't really mean us to go on, then?" Joseph asked.

"He dithered. We both did. So you were always in command of your own destiny."

It hadn't felt like it. There the children were, just as on the Italian frontier, under the benevolent control of military; but this time nobody's enthusiasm suggested that something was bound to happen. They were merely well looked after, and visited occasionally by the smiling Captain Mayne, who told them to be patient as if he had never realized that a divine impatience was their inspiring force. The only contact with the world of their imagination was that they were living in tents on the edge of the desert.

And that hard, lion-colored surface was all which separated them from Palestine? Couldn't they walk there? Hadn't all the conquerors of ancient history crossed the Sinai desert? In the gray of dawn, stealthily, an advance party set out with their water and the unexpended portion of the day's rations. Their tents were outside the military cantonments. No one saw them leave but the prowling Egyptian children — sleepers and scavengers who rose from the dust and accompanied them, mocking, capering and gesticulating obscenely. The little column marched on unconcerned, following a straight course across packed sand and gravel never disturbed by the wheel tracks of any of the armies which had cautiously hastened from Egypt into Syria. The palms of the Canal vanished over the horizon. The native children scuttled back to the safety of mud walls.

"I am always surprised that you found us," Horsha said.

"Oh, it wasn't difficult! The trouble was that I had been away. So you had two days' start, and the little wretches you left behind wouldn't say a word. But I knew exactly what you would do. Didn't I tell you that I, too, was very young then? You would march on Jerusalem by your compass."

That was their route when Mayne and his hastily borrowed cavalrymen discovered them marching east-northeast through the midday heat, stumbling, their water gone, but still in good close order. They reckoned to cover another five miles of deadly emptiness before they collapsed.

No more resistance was possible for the general. There were two good reasons for that. One was the children's determination. They could not be guarded night and day to prevent some further lunacy. The other was their chivalry. The beauty of the relationship between girls and boys was so obvious that it had never occurred to Mayne or his general that anyone could object to the proximity of their various tents. But there was no keeping out the chaplains and the welfare workers, and it was their business to protest.

The plaguing of the general increased and, like Pharaoh, he had no reasonable solution. He might have invented an excuse for putting one or two children on the new military railway to Haifa, but not twenty-six — for he was only the commander of a base. He would have had the politicians down on him, let alone Allenby's Chief of Staff.

"Did he put the blame on you?" Aviva asked.

"Only damned my eyes in a general way. There were no real reproaches. We were both emotionally affected by your spirit, you see. You had to go to Palestine. Had to go. That was why at last I gave you my promise that you should."

It had been a knightly gathering, though the banners and shields were there only in the eye of imagination. The children were drawn up in the space between the tents and took oath, eager-eyed and solemn-faced, that they would not leave the camp without permission. And in his turn Mayne gave his word of honor that he would lead them to Palestine.

"You were tremendously impressive," Horsha assured him. "You, the young Count of the Empire who had galloped up to our rescue!"

"Then it was my turn to radiate a confidence I didn't have," Mayne answered. "I remember wondering how on earth I was going to keep my word."

But the fact that he had given it was a third good reason for the general, who provided all that was in his power to provide — two lorries and rations, a week's leave for the importunate Captain Mayne and a pass which would take the whole party to Palestine so long as no one questioned it. And he wrote privately to the Chief Rabbi of Jerusalem, for he could not think of anyone else to arrange the children's reception.

"We addressed him as Your Grace," said Mayne with a chuckle. "His rank, we reckoned, must be equivalent to an archbishop. And we told the general's pet runner, who carried the letter, to be extra polite and mind his saluting."

The still Canal had just ceased to reflect the stars when the two lorries drove down it towards the desert track. The children were the first band of illegal immigrants, although, as in all their journey, they had no thought of breaking any law. Where there was none, their spirit supplied it.

Mayne, the drivers and their mates caught the infection of romance. They felt themselves explorers, and would have deliberately supplied adventure if there had not been enough in reality. The crossing of deserts by motor vehicles was then too new to be taken for granted. The lorries on their solid tires ponderously ground and bumped over irregularities of surface. Halts were frequent, and the running repairs of heavy complexity and doubtful value. The children were battered and bruised by the journey; but at night, wrapped in blankets on the sand, they abandoned themselves utterly to sleep — sleep which all their lives, said Joseph and Aviva, they remembered for its quality of peace. The next day they would have conquered.

Of this they were so sure that Mayne, against his better judgment, resumed the journey with a single lorry; the other had to be abandoned to await a tow to workshops. But even springs and axles obeyed the children. The remaining truck crept stolidly north until, instead of lonely shepherds, they saw huts with men and women sitting idle after harvest at the doors. Patches of sparse stubble began to appear among the scrub and dry thorn.

Was it at last Palestine? Well, no one could say for certain. But it was decidedly not Egypt. Two hours later the lorry limped into an Arab village and approached a group of European colonists, deep-eyed and sunburned, who waited patiently and could not yet see what precious freight was packed on blankets under the canvas hood.

Again the children asked if they had come to Palestine, and this time, though maps and politicians might be unwilling to commit themselves, history had no doubt. Mayne could not remember what he answered. He was very anxious to hand over his charge and retreat into the desert before civilians and military could overwhelm him with embarrassing questions. Nor could he trust himself to speak, for long war and sacrifice and promise, children and place and the ancient sanctities of Jew and Christian were of profound emotional power.

"You said," Aviva reminded him, " 'This is Beersheba. I must leave you now.' "